Captive

By Leda Swann

LEDA SWANN

Captive

AVON

An Imprint of HarperCollinsPublishers

CAPTIVE. Copyright © 2009 by Leda Swann. All rights reserved. Printed in the United States of America. No part of this book may be used or reproduced in any manner whatsoever without written permission except in the case of brief quotations embodied in critical articles and reviews. For information, address HarperCollins Publishers, 10 East 53rd Street, New York, NY 10022.

HarperCollins books may be purchased for educational, business, or sales promotional use. For information, please write: Special Markets Department, HarperCollins Publishers, 10 East 53rd Street, New York, NY 10022.

FIRST AVON PAPERBACK EDITION PUBLISHED 2009.

Designed by Diahann Sturge

Library of Congress Cataloging-in-Publication Data
Swann, Leda.
    Captive / Leda Swann.—1st ed.
        p. cm.
    ISBN 978-0-06-167239-2 (acid-free paper)
    I. Title.
    PS3619.I548C37 2009
    813'.6—dc22   2008043294

09 10 11 12   OV/RRD   10 9 8 7 6 5 4 3 2 1

One

Naples, Italy—1876

What is the opposite of déjà vu?

Louisa Clemens stopped in consternation barely a few paces into the parlor. The room felt peculiarly different, as if she had never set foot in it before. After working six years for the Winterbottoms, she knew every inch of their parlor—the blue carpet patterned with roses, the chintz-covered sofas, the ormolu clock on the mantel, and the glass case full of ferns in the corner of the bay window—yet she felt as if she had never been there before.

Plastering a façade of normality over her sudden feeling of strangeness, something different caught Louisa's eye, and she turned her head toward the side of the room where a man stood unabashedly staring at her. He was definitely not the sort of man she would expect to see in the Winterbottoms' parlor, ensconced among all their other guests. She faltered once again, the sensation of foreignness overcoming her.

It was his eyes that she noticed first, piercing eyes transfixing her with a gaze that seemed to search out *all* her secrets and leave nothing hidden. They were dark gray, the color of cold English skies and frozen cobblestones, with only the barest hint of the deep, mysterious ink of midnight.

The rest of the company assembled in the room may just as well have been invisible for all the notice Louisa could spare them. Next to him, everyone else seemed utterly insignificant. He was a tempest, a hurricane, a force so powerful that it slammed against her chest until she could hardly draw a breath. Against a nature as strong as his, she would have no chance of resistance.

That was why the room had seemed so strange to her—because *he* was in it. His mere presence had transformed the Winterbottoms' parlor into a room of mystery, a place Louisa no longer recognized.

She shivered in her light cotton gown, drew her Indian shawl closely around her shoulders, and turned her head away from danger, continuing toward the mother of the young children she chaperoned. Even though she could no longer see him, Louisa could feel the force of his gaze on her, stripping her bare. She knew that she had all of his attention. Everything about him was focused on her, and only on her.

"Ah, Miss Clemens, there you are." Mrs. Winterbottom bustled cheerfully toward Louisa, her mahogany ringlets bouncing under her cap. "I was just telling our guests about my little cherubs and here you are with them both. You have impeccable timing."

Though still shaken by the peculiar feeling that lingered in her spine and the directness of the stranger's gaze, Louisa smiled perfunctorily at her employer. "Prudence, Hester," she said gently to the two identical twin girls who trotted at her side, "make a curtsy for your mama."

The girls did as they were bid, holding out their puffed skirts and sinking into a pretty curtsy, all the while sneaking wide-eyed peeks at the guests, and at the gray-eyed stranger in particular.

Louisa was not surprised at their curiosity. Even in this urbane and sophisticated household, where businessmen from many parts of the world visited Mr. Winterbottom, a guest like this was most unusual.

She sneaked a look at him herself out of the corner of her eye, not wishing to be caught by his gaze again, or to let him guess her interest. Everything about him was different. For a start, his skin was tanned to a deep brown, even far darker than the Italians among whom they lived. His high cheekbones lent his face a severe grace, and his hair fell in thick, black waves nearly to his shoulders instead of being neatly pomaded to sit flat against his head, the style preferred by most gentlemen.

His clothing was as unusual as his looks. Though his navy

blue jacket was cut in the usual style, it was richly decorated with heavy gold and red embroidery, and his trousers were pristine white rather than the more usual black. He wore a round, red, high cap with a black tassel that made him appear even more exotic, while all the other men in the room were bareheaded, having removed their hats upon coming inside. He stood out among the crowd of Europeans as a wild hawk would stand out in a farmyard full of domesticated chickens.

The girls had dipped into a low curtsy. "Good girls," Mrs. Winterbottom said approvingly as they straightened up again. "Now then, come and hug your mama."

The pair obediently suffered a hug from their mother without undue wriggling. Inwardly, Louisa breathed a sigh of relief. Mrs. Winterbottom was a kindhearted woman and possessed the best of tempers, but the one thing she hated above all else was having her fine silk dress ruffled—particularly when she was in the company of handsome guests, as she was this evening.

There was no denying that the man who had caught Louisa's attention was handsome in an exotic way. He was much more attractive than the pallid young Englishman with ginger sideburns paying court to one of Mrs. Winterbottom's friends, and even more good-looking than the dark-haired and debonair Italian count flirting outrageously with the elderly—and terribly wealthy—dowager in the corner.

Louisa glanced over at Mr. Winterbottom as he poured

sherry at the sideboard. Next to the visitor, even Mr. Winterbottom looked pale and uninteresting. She noticed for the first time that his hairline was starting to recede and that, despite his firmly buttoned waistcoat, good living had given him a slight paunch. In contrast, the stranger looked to be all hard muscle with barely an ounce of fat on him, strong and untamed, and quite out of place in this quiet, gentile setting.

Seeming quite unperturbed by the dangerous allure that hung about the stranger like a miasma, Mrs. Winterbottom guided her daughters toward him. "Come, my dears, make a curtsy to our guests, especially to Mr. Khair, who has come all the way from Morocco to meet you."

"Khair Bey, if you please. That is my name in my own country."

His voice matched the rest of him, deep and rich, so different from the whining nasal tones of most English visitors. More than that, it was his manner of speaking, the soft lilt of his voice not found in Louisa's usual circles, that set him apart. Even his diction was perfect, though colored with a marked foreign accent.

The girls curtsied, their eyes fixed on him with utter fascination. Louisa almost smiled to think that she was not the only female in the room to feel his power.

He bowed and continued speaking. "Such beauty have I rarely seen in thousands of miles of travel across oceans and distant lands. I am captive in your presence."

Though perfectly polite, he pushed the boundaries of good manners when greeting someone for the first time. A simple "Enchanted, I'm sure" would have more than sufficed.

The two girls to whom he spoke blushed with his words, their eyes wide with the exoticness of the visitor. And as he spoke, Louisa knew with unreasoned but unswerving conviction that, while he spoke to the girls in her charge, he was actually addressing her.

Hester—or was it Prudence?—gave a tiny giggle, but quickly repressed it after a stern look from her mama.

Mrs. Winterbottom seated herself on the sofa and carefully arranged her skirts by her side. Her daughters arranged themselves in similar fashion by their mother, knowing she would never tolerate anything higgledy-piggledy in this most orderly of parlors. With a sideways glance at the intriguing stranger, Louisa remained standing just inside the doorway, ready if she were needed for some minor emergency—perhaps tea spilled on Prudence's new gown or incipient tears from the easily upset Hester. Her services would then be needed to change the gown or to wipe away the tears before delivering her charges back to their proud mama in pristine condition once more.

For once she was pleased to stay in the parlor for a few minutes while Mrs. Winterbottom showed off her daughters to the visitors. Though all the guests would no doubt utterly ignore Louisa's silent presence by the door, at least she could sneak the odd glance at Khair Bey when he was looking elsewhere. She had never before met a man who had interested her so much at first sight.

To her surprise, however, Khair Bey immediately bowed in front of her. "And this charming young lady is . . . ?" he inquired of his host.

Mrs. Winterbottom raised her eyebrows at his query, but did not rise from the sofa. "That is Louisa Clemens," she said dismissively, with a wave of her hand, "my dear angels' nursery maid."

Clearly Khair Bey did not understand from Mrs. Winterbottom's reply that Louisa was not an equal in this household, but merely a servant. Or if he did understand, he deliberately ignored her lowly status. His next question was aimed directly at her, once again in that forthright manner. "Are you a relative of my hosts?"

Louisa gave Mrs. Winterbottom an awkward glance. Her employer was almost scowling at her guest's breach of etiquette. One simply did not notice servants when in polite company, and one certainly did not speak to them as equals or ask to be introduced. It was as if he'd asked for an introduction to one of the potted plants that stood at attention in the dining room.

Louisa had discovered soon enough that she was fair game for the gentlemen visitors of the house to pester in the hallways, in the garden, or whenever they could get her alone. But they never acknowledged her in company—not even if they had been vowing their undying love to her or begging her to warm their bed not half an hour before in the rose garden.

But Khair Bey was talking directly to her—and in the best parlor, too. Never having been placed in such a situation before, she was not sure what to do. Politeness meant she could not refuse to answer him, but as a servant, she could not enter into a conversation with a visitor as if she were one of the guests. The very notion was absurd. She could see no way out of her dilemma.

Mrs. Winterbottom rescued her with a little sniff of displeasure. "No, she is no relation."

Khair Bey gave Louisa the merest hint of a smile before turning to his hostess. "I apologize if I have disturbed you by asking, but in Morocco the care of our children is a task that is never left to strangers. Only the closest relatives or the most trustworthy of friends are permitted to have a hand in their upbringing. That is why I thought perhaps she was a relative— maybe your unmarried sister."

Mr. Winterbottom gave a genial shake of his head as he passed a glass of sherry to Khair Bey. A successful fabric merchant who had traveled through much of Europe and even into India and other parts, he had no doubt come across many customs stranger than this. "No offense taken. I knew the girl's father. I did some business with him a number of years ago, when he was in a better situation. We took her in some years ago, when the girls were born. She's become quite a member of the family."

Louisa allowed herself a small smile at his words. Maybe that was stretching the truth just a little. She was their nursery maid, a servant. She was paid a wage to perform a task—that was the extent of her interaction with her employers. But she loved the children and they loved her, the family was a happy, well-ordered one, and she was content with her position.

Khair Bey looked at her over the top of his sherry glass, but made no attempt to drink. "Delightful, utterly delightful."

Once again, Louisa knew that the words were meant for her, and only for her.

She stood up a little straighter in her post by the doorway, willing herself not to let any sign of pleased vanity escape her at his notice. Judging by his clothing, he was a very wealthy merchant or the like, and she was nothing but a nursery maid. While the Winterbottoms always treated her with the utmost respect, she had received plenty of the wrong sort of attention from their friends and acquaintances—men who thought it was their right to be entertained by any servant who took their fancy, who assumed that her lowly station came accompanied with low morals, and who tried to buy her virtue. All of them had been rebuffed with the same sweet smile that—if they had looked closely, they would have realized—never reached her eyes.

Louisa did not want to know whatever path Khair Bey might take to fulfill his desires, for he would not find a willing accomplice in her. She would prefer to be spared the pain of having to refuse him, too, if he tried to come courting. He seemed to be the kind of man she could almost like.

She stood and watched as he made much of Prudence and Hester, admiring their matching yellow and white dresses and applauding loudly at their halting performance on the pianoforte. Mrs. Winterbottom beamed with pride at every compliment he paid them. Certainly he had found a way into their mother's heart. She looked as if she wanted to throw her arms around him and kiss him for recognizing the superior sweetness and intelligence of her darling offspring.

But although his attention seemed focused on the children, it was Louisa to whom his gaze continually returned. His watchful eyes followed her as she handed Hester a clean pocket handkerchief and retied a stray hair ribbon for Prudence. Even when she stood out of the way at her post near the door, she could feel his eyes on her, taking in every move she made. He watched her as a cat would fix its gaze on a fat little mouse that unwittingly strayed into its path.

It was clear that Louisa would have to be wary of him. He had the look of a man who was used to getting whatever he wanted—and he was eyeing her as if he were parched with thirst and she was a long, cold glass of fresh springwater. She shivered slightly, whether from the cool evening air and her distance from the fire, or from something altogether less familiar.

"Will the children be joining us for dinner?" Though his voice was deep and soft, it carried an authority all its own.

Once again, Louisa noticed that his rhythm of speaking made him stand out from the crowd. She could listen to him talking all day and not tire of the soft lilt to his speech.

Mr. Winterbottom, to whom the query was addressed, looked almost pained at the idea. "The girls eat in the nursery—bread, milk, and other wholesome foods; nothing too rich to upset their delicate young stomachs."

Mrs. Winterbottom turned beseeching eyes on her husband. "Surely just this once they could eat downstairs with us. We are a smallish party tonight and they have been so well behaved. Our other guests will not mind. And if Mr. Khair, I mean Khair Bey, has no objection . . ."

Indeed, Khair Bey had no objection. "Their nursery maid must stay for dinner as well," he proclaimed in a regal fashion. "She can keep watch over them. That way you can be sure they will be no trouble at all."

"What a capital idea!" Mrs. Winterbottom clapped her hands together. "Come, Louisa, you must stay and dine with us tonight. You can mind the girls just as well down here for once."

Louisa swallowed hard, her breath caught with surprise at the proposition. She had been counting on taking her leave very shortly with the excuse that the girls' dinner would be ready in the nursery. In the six years that she had been their nursery maid, she could count on the fingers of one hand the number of times they had invited the children to dine with them. And never before had they asked her to join them.

She shot a glance at Khair Bey. As she had expected, his eyes were gleaming with triumph. He had wanted to dine with her, and he planned it so that she could not refuse.

She directed a brief scowl in his direction. Whatever he baited his hook with, she would not bite. "If you wish me to."

"We all wish it," Khair Bey confirmed.

She shrugged the feeling of his voice from her shoulders. Everything he said, however innocuous it was, sounded obscenely like a caress.

Mrs. Winterbottom shot her a curious look. "If you will not be uncomfortable, that is. I know you are not dressed for dinner, but none of us will mind."

Louisa felt her face grow hot, suddenly aware of how ungracious she must appear. "I will be glad to stay. Thank you for your kind invitation."

Mrs. Winterbottom beamed. "Good, that's settled then. All three of you shall dine with us."

Khair Bey managed to organize affairs so that Louisa was seated next to him at dinner. Somehow she wasn't surprised. He was clearly experienced at getting exactly what he wanted, and it was becoming increasingly obvious that he had his eye on her.

Throughout the first course, she tried her best to ignore him, instead attending assiduously to Hester on her other side. But as the soup bowls were being removed, a significant nod by Mrs. Winterbottom awakened her sense of obligation. The children were not too young to be taught good manners, and as their nursery maid she ought to set a good example. She turned to Khair Bey with a pleasant smile. "Are you staying long in Naples, Khair Bey?"

He twirled the stem of his empty wineglass between his fingers. He had refused wine and asked instead for water. His nails were cut short and square and his palms looked calloused, as if he had labored hard and long with his hands. "As long as it takes me to conclude my business here." His teeth were white and even as he smiled—the teeth of a predator.

Louisa suppressed a shiver. She was allowing her fancy to run away with her. He was nothing but a businessman, come to enjoy an informal dinner with her employers. "And what business do you have here in Italy?"

His eyes narrowed fractionally. "I have many business interests."

She arched one eyebrow at him. Clearly, he was a master of the polite nonanswer. "Please, do not divulge any state secrets on my account." Her smile took any sting from her words. "But if you prefer to converse with your other neighbor," and she nodded to indicate the racy young widow seated on the other side of him, "then I will be happy to oblige you."

A discreet—and timely—tug on her sleeve made her turn back to Hester, who required some assistance to cut her portion of roast beef.

The moment she was finished, he reclaimed her attention. "It would be impolite of me to monopolize Mrs. Tofts with my conversation. She, too, has another neighbor who is eagerly awaiting her notice."

Mrs. Tofts looked rather glum at this, but she turned back to the elderly colonel seated on her other side with only a slight moue of disappointment.

Louisa gave Khair Bey another slight smile and began to eat her dinner in silence, determined to let *him* make the conversation if he wished to talk. She had tried once already and had been rebuffed.

Khair Bey looked at her for some moments before he spoke again. "Have you been a nursery maid for long?"

She saw no reason to prevaricate, as he had done with her. "For nearly six years now."

"You must have been very young when you started."

"I was sixteen—quite old enough to be useful."

"You are a long way from home, my pretty little English rose." His voice was low, too soft for the other guests to hear. "One does not often see such pink cheeks and fair hair in the south of Italy."

She shrugged, refusing to let him turn her head with his easy compliments. Her pale skin and fair hair were merely accidents of her birth, nothing she could take credit for. "The English climate was no good for my chest. I took the post with the Winterbottoms to travel with them into Italy. It is so much warmer and drier here."

"You prefer the Italian climate?"

She nodded. "England is always so cold and damp. I'm not looking forward to returning there—except to see my brother and sisters, of course. I miss them all greatly, but I don't miss the cough that plagued me through every English winter."

"If you like the heat, you will love my country." He picked up her hand and brought it to his lips before he spoke again. "Our houses are built not to shelter us from the cold, but to shield us from the heat of the sun. My house has a paved court-yard shaded by orange trees, where fountains cool the air and provide a soothing music. Even in the depths of winter it is never cold, unless you travel into the mountains. You will be happy there."

Louisa smiled a little uneasily at his presumption as she withdrew her hand from his clasp. Even if his house had a thousand courtyards, she was unlikely to see a single one. When Mr. Winterbottom's business interests required him to go overseas, he generally traveled alone, usually leaving his wife and children at their house in Naples. Since arriving there to work for the Winterbottoms, she had never left Naples. "It sounds very pretty. You must miss your home." Her voice, though still pleasant, had lost its warmth, and she edged away from him slightly. He made her feel trapped, as if he was slowly but surely driving her into a corner from which she could not escape.

"But Morocco is not all fountains and orange trees," he

warned, his tone darkening. "Parts of it are still as wild and untamed as they were more than a thousand years ago. There is a desert in the south where there is nothing but sand, yellow sand, with dunes that march to the horizon. The heat there is so fierce that no man can withstand it. Even camels, who are made for the heat and can survive without drinking for weeks at a time, cannot survive for long there."

He captured her gaze with his own. "Morocco, and the people who live there, can be as gentle as a lamb or as savage as a lion, depending on the way they are treated in return."

"They are the same as any other people then," she replied, a little tartly. Did he think he would frighten her with tales of Moroccan ferocity? No tales of barbaric cruelty from other lands could upset her. She had suffered worse than he could imagine at the hands of her own countrymen, in the so-called civilized country of England. As a child, she had been put in the workhouse and nearly starved to death through no fault of her own, but because of her father's business debts.

If he thought she was a hothouse flower that wilted at the first sign of adversity, he would find himself sorely mistaken. Though she might look pale and have a weak chest, the heart that beat inside it was stronger than many a grown man's.

His eyes narrowed at her tone of voice. Taking a mouthful of roast beef, he chewed it thoughtfully and swallowed. "Have you been with the same family all this time?"

"Since I came to Naples, yes, I have. The girls are fond of me and I am of them." She gave a tiny sigh. "But they are at the age where they need a governess more than a nursery maid. I fear I shall have to look for another post shortly— hopefully another English family here. I would be sad to have to leave Italy."

"You will not teach them?"

She winced at his question; he had touched on a sore point. "I would if I could," she admitted, "but I fear I would make a woeful governess. My own education came to a premature end. I could no more teach them geography or French than I could fly. I can read and write, and keep simple accounts, but that is all. I do not have a single elegant accomplishment. Dancing, painting, and even playing the piano are quite beyond me."

"Come to Morocco and teach my children."

"You have children?" A spurt of anger arose in her breast. She should have guessed that he was married with a family— the majority of her most ardent admirers were. Still, she was disappointed in him. For a few moments she had almost liked him. It was a wonder how he had the gall to openly pursue her when he had a wife and children waiting at home—and under his hosts' own roof! He was no better than the rest of them.

"Not yet." He grinned easily at her. "But together we can quickly remedy that small problem."

She suppressed the guilty pleasure she received at hearing he was not married, but her throat flushed at the rather forward proposal to remedy his lack of children. Wed or not, it made no difference to her. He was a bey—a man of wealth, power, and influence. Such men wanted her for only one thing, and she had no interest in giving it to them. Though she was only a nursery maid, she had as much pride as a duchess—probably more, since she had to fight for hers so often. "I don't think so," she replied in her most quelling tone. "I am not interested in any such proposition."

Her words were a lie. Khair Bey interested her more than any other man she had met in the Winterbottoms' parlor—or anywhere. He had treated her not as a servant but as an equal, with politeness and deference—a courtesy she was not used to. The orange trees and fountains he had described sounded so beautiful, and she would love to look out over a sea of sand from the back of a camel, with a handsome man such as Khair Bey sharing her saddle.

She gave herself a little shake. Such wishes were mere daydreams, and she was too sensible to indulge in futile dreaming for long.

Though the footman had not yet begun to clear the dishes for the dessert that would follow, she turned her head firmly away from Khair Bey's improper conversation and attended instead to Hester's dropped napkin.

Khair Bey looked with some amusement at the back of his pretty dinner companion's head, but she pretended to be oblivious to his presence. Only the tide of creeping color that suffused the back of her neck hinted that she was not ignorant of, nor immune to, his proximity.

She was so prickly, this little English rose he had found hiding in the south of Italy. From the moment he had seen her glide into the parlor, he had been utterly transfixed by her ethereal loveliness. Her skin was so pale it was almost translucent, and her glorious hair was the color of his homeland's desert sands. One sweet smile at the young children in her charge, and he was utterly enraptured. Beauty was always welcome in a woman, but such a genuine sweetness of temper was infinitely rarer and more precious. Her company at dinner had confirmed his first impressions of her. Though she tried hard to feign a prickly exterior, her prickles were clearly only skin deep. He knew that underneath she was all sweet woman.

How fortunate for him that she was not related to his hosts. Although it would be bad form to seduce her while he was under their roof, she was a servant, and seducing servants was not unheard of, nor unforgivable. If she had been Mrs. Winterbottom's younger sister or niece, as he had first suspected, he would have had to tread much more carefully. He did not want to risk losing the lucrative business he was engaged in with Mr. Winterbottom merely for the sake of a woman—his community depended on him too much to carelessly jeopardize their welfare. He might even have been forced to offer to take her as his wife, if he had been caught in an awkward situation with her. Entanglements like that were best avoided whenever possible.

He let a smile curve his lips. As it was, he would have no such difficulties in his path. Alone and without powerful friends as she was, she would fall into his hands as easily as picking a ripe date. The idea pleased him—he did not have the patience or the temperament for long courtships.

He carried on a desultory conversation with his other neighbor at the dinner table. Ordinarily he would have considered Mrs. Tofts a pretty woman, and he would have been suitably grateful to his hosts for pairing him with her. Tonight, however, he had little patience for her practiced flirtations, the way she pretended to hang on his every word as if it were gold, or the manner in which she accidentally brushed against him at every opportunity.

Women such as Mrs. Tofts could be found everywhere he turned—European women without companions, or bored with the men they had married, seeking to find entertainment in another man's embrace. Though he despised their lack of morals, he was hypocrite enough to take advantage of them. He saw no reason to refuse what they offered so freely.

His looks were sufficiently exotic in most European countries for him to stand out from the crowd, but he was realistic enough to understand that his face was not the main reason women flocked around him. His fabled wealth was at least as great an attraction, not to mention his generosity to his bed partners—his well-known habit of leaving a pretty bracelet or other trinket to remember him by ensured that his advances were seldom rebuffed. A rich man with a reputation for largesse was—for most women he had met outside his homeland—a prize worth having.

Any other night, he would have made an assignation with Mrs. Tofts for later in the evening and spent the night pleasuring her and being pleasured in return. If she had delighted him sufficiently, he might even have repeated the invitation. Her bosom was certainly plump and full—her dress left little to his imagination—and judging by the breathy sighs she had made in his ear all evening, her pink pussy would be wet and hungry for the taste of his big cock. She would no doubt give him a good ride, and earn her parting gift with her enthusiasm, if not with her finesse.

But tonight Mrs. Tofts' rather obvious charms left him cold. Too much of her was on display for anyone to see: her hair, her arms, her breasts, even a hint of ankle. The more that was on show, the colder it left him. There would be no mystery in bedding her, no discovery in taking off her clothes, removing her inhibitions, and coaxing her into his bed.

Louisa, the pretty nursery maid, was another story. Her dress modestly covered her bosom and even her beautiful hair was mostly covered under her plain cap. She was dressed more like his own countrywomen than anyone else in the room. Women in Morocco believed that a little mystery did not diminish a woman's allure but rather added to it—and he agreed with them wholeheartedly. Pretty Louisa was obviously of the same mind, taking care to hide all her treasures from view. Persuading her to his bed would be like unwrapping a delicious package, a gift meant only for him.

His mouth watered with anticipation. He took another swallow of water and grimaced at its muddy taste. Though as a matter of principle he did not drink wine or spirits if he could politely refuse to do so, he might have to change his ways if he was to remain much longer in Italy. The water here was far removed from the crystal clear springwater he was used to.

No matter—why should he care about the quality of the water in Italy when the quality of the women was inarguable? He had not met so tempting a morsel as Louisa for months. Already he could almost feel the softness of her hair, and the firm thrust of her breasts against his palms. Her thighs would be plump and soft, and when he slid his hand right up to her private parts, her pussy would be covered in fine down, and dripping with welcoming moisture. Though she would try to deny it with her words, her body would tell its own story. She would be ready for him—more than ready—and by the time he took her, she would want him as much as he already wanted her.

How tight she would be against him as he slowly entered her, first with one finger, and then two, getting her used to the sensation of being opened, of having her body discovered by a man. Then, when she had become accustomed to the new sensation of being stretched, he would move on top of her and position himself right at the entrance of her pussy. She would be almost too tight for his cock, but he would push into her slowly, breaching her maidenhead, opening her wider with every thrust, until he was buried in her up to the hilt.

He took another swig of the brackish water to cool his brain. The evening was only just beginning and already his balls were aching with the thought of fucking her. Usually he steered clear of virgins—they were more trouble than they were worth—but he would make an exception for Louisa. He would be the first man she took into her bed and into her body, and he would teach her to find joy.

How glad he was that he had decided to remain in Naples to conclude his business. He had a great many beautiful woven carpets to sell, and although Mr. Winterbottom was only one of the Italian merchants who were anxious to buy them, he had a reputation for fair and honest dealings. So Khair Bey had accepted the man's hospitality, and with it an unspoken agreement to give him the first rights of refusal over his choicest offerings.

It was his good luck that Mr. Winterbottom had such a delight to offer him in return.

The remainder of the dinner passed with an interminable slowness. Mrs. Tofts made every effort to monopolize his attention over dessert, and Louisa refused to be drawn back into a conversation with him. Though she was attracted to him, she was determined to resist it. Poor young woman, he thought. This was a battle she could never win. He would not allow her to maintain her resistance for long.

Now that he had made the decision to seduce her, he was impatient to get on with the business of the evening so he could be free to pursue his personal interests. Every minute he spent in her company without being able to cover her soft neck with nibbling kisses or stroke her naked breasts and belly, was a minute wasted. When he wanted something, he wanted it immediately. He shifted uncomfortably in his chair, surreptitiously adjusting himself beneath the tablecloth to give himself the extra room he needed. Just thinking about taking the girl to his bed had made his cock harder than was comfortable.

He was almost out of patience altogether when Mrs. Winterbottom arose from the table. Finally, this is what he had been waiting for—the signal for the ladies to depart. Immediately he felt more at ease, knowing that dinner was almost over. Despite having dined with a number of European families over the past few weeks, he could not get used to men and women eating together at the same table, and the women with their faces uncovered. He was traditional enough that such a display never sat well with him.

Dining with a woman was meant to be an intimate affair, not this promiscuous intermingling of male and female bodies around a table. It should be just the two of them, sitting on cushions around a low table. He would hand-feed her tender pieces of seasoned lamb and sweet figs. Then, when they had eaten their fill, he would lie her down on the cushions and make love to her until their hunger for each other was assuaged . . .

He greedily watched Louisa as she stood, her back kept ostentatiously to him. Her display of indifference could not fool him. She was intrigued by him—he could sense her interest. Though she tried to fix her attention elsewhere, her gaze always returned to him, particularly when she thought he was looking elsewhere. He had caught her attention, and that was the first and most critical step in any seduction. With a girl as young and inexperienced as she was, the rest ought to be child's play.

Soon—soon he would have her in his arms and touch her as he wanted to, as he needed to.

The children were already yawning and sleepily rubbing their eyes. His sense of anticipation heightened. Louisa would surely not linger in the drawing room with the other women, but would take the girls off to bed. Once her two charges were settled for the night, it would leave her free to be taken to his bed.

Louisa's hips swayed provocatively under her modest gown as she left the room. She knew he was watching her, the minx, and she wanted to entice him. Damn it all, he was already so enticed that his cock felt as though it would burst out of his trousers. She had no need to provoke him further.

He breathed a sigh of relief when the door closed behind them and the men were left alone. Without Louisa tantalizingly close by his side, without her perfume in his nostrils, he would finally be able to concentrate on arranging the sale of the carpets that had been entrusted to his care.

He passed the port to the man next to him without filling his glass.

The man looked at him curiously, his bloodshot eyes blinking blearily as he filled his own glass to the brim. "You don't drink port?"

"I prefer to conduct my business with a clear head."

The man took a deep swig from his glass before refilling it and passing the bottle on. "I never trust a fellow who won't drink with me." His voice was slurred. "Specially not a rum-looking fellow like you. You're too black by half for my liking . . ." His words tailed off into an indistinct muttering.

"Then it is lucky I am not doing business with you," Khair Bey replied equably. There was no point in getting into an argument at his host's table, even when faced with outright rudeness.

"Jack, move over for a moment, will you?" Mr. Winterbottom came over and displaced the sot, who wandered out of the dining room in a dazed torpor, clearly looking for somewhere to relieve himself.

Mr. Winterbottom's glass, Khair Bey noticed, was full of water like his own. His estimation of his host raised a notch. Only a fool clouded his wits with wine when business matters were on the table. "Thank you for inviting me to dinner. The food was very fine, as was the company."

"You are welcome." Mr. Winterbottom leaned forward and lowered his voice a trifle. "Now, about the matter of business we were to discuss tonight. You know I am interested in your goods and I will pay a fair price for them."

"I have heard you deal fairly."

Mr. Winterbottom accepted the words not as a compliment, but as his due. "I do. How many carpets can you put aside for me?"

Khair Bey shrugged. He had already decided to do business with the man or he would never have accepted his hospitality. "You may buy as many as you like, provided we can agree on the terms."

Mr. Winterbottom's eyes glinted with satisfaction at the ease of his triumph. "You will not regret it, I can assure you."

Khair Bey cut short his thanks with a wave of one hand. "I have one condition to the sale."

"And that is?" The light in Mr. Winterbottom's eyes turned from triumphant to suspicious.

"I have taken a fancy to Naples and would like to see more of it. Offer me a bed in your house for ten days, and you may buy as many carpets as you choose."

Mr. Winterbottom hesitated. "Is this anything to do with our nursery maid, Louisa?" he asked slowly. "I saw how you were looking at her this evening—as if you wanted to eat her."

Khair Bey looked him straight in the eye. "What business is it of yours?"

"Her father was an honest man and she is under my protection. I would not have her hurt in any way."

Khair Bey merely looked at him in silence, daring him to refuse.

Mr. Winterbottom was the first to look away. "Very well, you may stay with us as you wish." He beckoned to a footman standing in the corner and whispered instructions to him. "The maids will make a room ready for you."

"Thank you. You are very kind." Inside his heart was exulting. As their houseguest, he would have numerous opportunities to further his acquaintance with Louisa—and he would be sure to take maximum advantage of them. Mr. Winterbottom's compliance had just given him ten nights of having Louisa in his bed. That would be more than enough time to sate himself.

"And the price of the carpets?" Mr. Winterbottom queried. "What do you want per piece?"

His gratitude did not extend to giving Mr. Winterbottom a single price without considering the fineness of the weave. "I shall take you to the warehouse tomorrow where you can examine a selection of different grades. Once you are satisfied with the quality of the goods, we can agree on a final price for each grade."

Mr. Winterbottom looked as though he might protest, but Khair Bey was in no mood to dicker over the finer points of their deal tonight. He had more pressing matters on his mind, which he intended to draw to a satisfactory conclusion as soon as he could—tonight, if fortune favored him. "Now, if you will excuse me, would you kindly have a maid show me to my room? I have had a long day."

Two

Safely in the nursery, Louisa tucked a stray curl behind Prudence's ear and drew the coverlets up over Hester's shoulders. "Good night, sweethearts."

Exhausted from the unaccustomed excitement of dining with the grown-ups and staying up long past their usual bedtime, the young girls were already half asleep. Hester muttered something that might have been "good night" in reply. Prudence gave a gentle snore.

Louisa extinguished the gas lamps, leaving the room in darkness, and tiptoed out of the nursery.

Her room was conveniently located right next to the girls', so she could hear if they woke up and needed something in the night. Luckily for her, they were both sound sleepers and seldom disturbed her rest.

She liked the quiet time in the evenings when the children were settled in bed. Both the cook and the housekeeper had become good friends of hers, and once the children were asleep, she would often go to the housekeeper's sitting room and they would chat while she mended the girls' clothes or darned their stockings. Every so often, the housekeeper would bring out a bottle of sherry and they would each sip on a small glass to wash down a slice of leftover seed cake or a macaroon purloined from the kitchen. Mrs. Harris, the cook, made scrumptious macaroons—lovely crisp bites of sweetness that melted on your tongue. Despite the excellent dinner she had been served tonight, her mouth watered just thinking about them.

Given that she had never before been asked to dine at the same table as her employers, it was a shame that she had hardly tasted her dinner. Her neighbor at the table had made sure of that. Sitting beside him had completely robbed her of her appetite. Throughout the entire meal, he had looked at her as if he wanted to devour her instead of what was on his plate. How could she concentrate on eating when such danger stalked her?

The nearness of him had set her body tingling with awareness. She could tell exactly where he was, even when she was turned away and tending to the needs of one or the other of her small charges. It was almost as if she had an extra sense, one tuned only on him. No movement he made, however small, was beneath its notice.

She had never really understood before what made some young men—and older men, too—sniff around her skirts as if they were dogs in heat. None of them had ever so much as roused a spark of interest in her. Even the most persistent of them had left her completely unmoved.

But Khair Bey was different, and therein lay the danger. She would have to watch herself just as much as she would have to watch him. It was harder to resist a man's attentions when you secretly wanted to feel his hands under your skirts, stroking your thighs, delving between your legs to touch you where you burned for him . . .

She gave herself a little shake. There was no sense sitting alone in her little room obsessing about her reaction to a casual stranger. He would certainly waste no sleep over her. Company was what she needed tonight. Closing the door to her bedroom behind her, she made her way quietly down the servants' stairs and knocked on the housekeeper's parlor door.

Mrs. Botham ushered her in with a smile. "Come in and take a load off," she said, gesturing to the small chintz-covered sofa in the corner. "I've been that bothered and fussed all day, with preparing for the dinner party and then having to get the maids to make up a room for an unexpected guest at the last minute, my head is fair spinning. I was just having a bit of a tipple to put myself to rights." She gave a wink as she fetched another glass from the sideboard and poured a hefty swig of sherry into it. "And you know what they say about drinking alone."

"I can soon fix that," Louisa said, accepting the glass that

Mrs. Botham held out to her. She sipped appreciatively at the golden liquid, feeling its warmth seep into her bones. There was nothing quite like a glass of sweet sherry and pleasant company to unwind after a long day.

The two of them sat in companionable silence for a few moments, soaking in the peace of the late evening. Louisa took a couple more sips of the sherry and then put her glass down. "If I drink this too fast, all my stitches will be crooked." She gestured at the bag of mending she had brought with her. As nursery maid, she was also responsible for keeping the girls neatly and tidily dressed. Hester was a quiet little thing, but Prudence could be murder on her seams.

Mrs. Botham chuckled. "Be glad they're not boys. You'd not have a minute to yourself with all the holes they'd make in their clothes."

Louisa rummaged through the bag to see what was there. "It's only stockings to darn," she picked up her glass and took another large sip, "nothing that will show."

"Then you can have a drop more and no one will be the wiser." Mrs. Botham topped up Louisa's glass with a generous hand. "The butler will assume the company upstairs has gone through a little more than usual. That is, if he even notices a bottle's gone missing."

The sherry she'd already drunk was going to Louisa's head. She suppressed a giggle. "What a pair we are, getting tipsy together in your living room."

"I heard you had dinner in the drawing room tonight." Surprisingly, there was a note of pity in her voice. "I hope the gentry weren't too rough on you."

Louisa grimaced into her glass. "The girls were staying downstairs. I couldn't refuse."

"Just don't be getting ideas above your station," Mrs. Botham said with a grin. "The gentlemen in the parlor don't want a wife from below stairs."

"That's hardly likely. I might as well have been invisible for all the notice they paid me." *Except for Khair Bey*, she added silently to herself. He had been unfailingly—disturbingly—attentive.

"And how was the food at the high table tonight, my lady?" Mrs. Botham got up out of her chair and executed a rather clumsy curtsy before dissolving into laughter and collapsing back down again. "I hope you will still speak to us hoi polloi now that you have had a taste of the high life."

The sherry tasted better with every sip Louisa took. "I suppose I will," she said in a grand tone, somewhat spoiled by a loud hiccup in the middle. "But only if you are suitably subservient to me."

Then something that Mrs. Botham had mentioned earlier rang alarm bells in her head. "What was that you said about having to make up a room for an unexpected guest? I did not see anyone arrive during dinner. And all the guests were expected."

"Our unexpected guest was at the table tonight. A Moorish

man, the footman said. Skin the color of stewed tea, and dressed in a fancy, embroidered jacket, as if he were a prince."

Louisa's heart stopped and a lump arose in her throat. The housekeeper's words could mean only one thing. There had been only one Moorish man at dinner—the man who had wanted to devour her. "He's staying here? Khair Bey is staying here?"

"That's a funny kind of name, if you ask me. Khair Bey." The housekeeper pursed her lips in disapproval. "It's no kind of name for a Christian gentleman."

"I suspect he isn't one," Louisa said.

"Not a Christian or not a gentleman?"

She thought of the way he had eaten her up with his eyes, the way he had shamelessly maneuvered his hostess into seating her at the table with the rest of the guests, and then made sure he was seated beside her. And she remembered his comment about her teaching his children—the children he planned to make with her. "Neither."

"He's probably a Mussulman," Mrs. Botham gave an elaborate shudder, "one of them who worships false idols and sacrifices virgins at the full moon."

He hadn't seemed that interested in sacrificing her at a full moon. Other, more earthly things had definitely been occupying his thoughts. She giggled into her glass. Of course, he couldn't be sure she was a virgin, either.

"Or he'll be one of them who takes fifty wives and locks them all up together in a harem and never lets them out again.

Think of that. Fifty of you sharing one man, and all of you shut in together like rats in a cage. A woman would go barmy and scratch out her own eyes in a place like that."

"I'd rather have it the other way around. Fifty men to one of me," Louisa muttered, and then clapped her hand to her mouth with a moan of despair. "Did I just say that out loud?" She would never touch a drop of sherry again. It made her think wicked thoughts, and worse, it made her say them out loud. "Whatever will you think of me?"

Mrs. Botham reached over and filled up the sherry glasses one more time. "You only said what I was thinking. Mr. Botham, God rest his soul, was a sweet man most of the time—when he wasn't drinking, that is." She gave a snort. "But I wouldn't say no to fifty of them pretty Mussulmen locked up in a harem and all for me."

The pair of them doubled over with laughter at the idea of their very own Moorish harem.

"There'd be so many I wouldn't know what to do with them all," Louisa confessed. "I'd hardly know what to do with just one."

Mrs. Botham gave a sly wink. "I know what I'd do with the handsome ones alright. But as for the ugly ones?" She thought for a moment and her glance fell on Louisa's workbag. "I'd make the ugly ones darn my stockings."

"I'd pose them around the room and make them pretend they were Greek statues."

"Aren't Greek statues naked?"

Louisa felt herself blushing. She'd temporarily forgotten that minor detail. "Some of them wear draperies," she protested.

"I'd have the naked sort," Mrs. Botham said, her words slightly slurred. "They're much classier."

They tried to outdo each other thinking of the outrageous uses to which they could put fifty Mussulmen. It seemed only a few moments later that Louisa found the bottom of her sherry glass. She tipped it higher, but the golden liquid was indeed gone. Her head felt fuzzy and she was sure she could see two Mrs. Bothams sitting in the same chair—or were there two chairs? She blinked once or twice and gave her head a little shake, but her vision didn't clear. "I think I've had enough sherry," she muttered, getting to her feet. Her legs buckled unsteadily beneath her. "I'd best be getting back to my room while I can still walk."

Mrs. Botham held the sherry bottle out to her invitingly. "Another nightcap before you go?"

Louisa shook her head, and then regretted it. The movement unbalanced her still further and she had to grab on to the door frame to stop herself from toppling over. "No, thank you." She had never before consumed three glasses of sherry at one sitting. Or was it four? She had lost count. They had gone on quite a bender. "I really have to go."

Mrs. Botham waved her away, the bottle of sherry still in her hand. "Off you go, then," she said genially. "I'm gonna have jusht a little more before I turn in."

Louisa tiptoed along the corridor to the servant's staircase.

Judging by the noise from the other wing, the guests were still in the drawing room, no doubt sipping tea and making light conversation while the ladies showed off their accomplishments on the pianoforte or the harp.

She wondered with whom Khair Bey would be conversing, whose form he would be lovingly caressing with those dark gray eyes of his, and whose flirtations he would be responding to. He attracted women like honey attracted ants—she had seen the way the woman seated on his other side at dinner had tried to monopolize his conversation. Not that she cared, of course. He was free to flirt with whomever he liked.

The euphoria of the alcohol was wearing off now that she was alone in the dimly lit corridor, and the thought of Khair Bey flirting with another woman was enough to make her quite dismal. She hurried away from the noise of merriment and climbed up the staircase to the nursery.

Hester and Prudence were sound asleep. They did not even stir when she stumbled over the hearth rug as she entered. Their soft, even breaths carried through the night and she stood still just to enjoy listening to them. How she would love to have children of her own one day. Children she could love unreservedly and with all her heart, knowing that she would not have to leave them as soon as they were old enough to need a governess rather than a nursery maid—children who were hers.

Of course, she had to have a husband first, and there weren't any likely candidates for that position. The men who chased her were only interested in one thing—and it didn't include marriage. Occasionally, a valet visiting with his master might show her some attention, but only in a very desultory way. Not one of them had shown the slightest interest in falling in love with her and marrying her.

Dearly as she wanted a family of her own, she had not yet reached that stage of desperation whereby she would have a child on any terms, with or without a husband. She would have no way of supporting herself and a child except by accepting charity from her brother and sisters. Even if she became an unwed mother, she knew that they would gladly support her, but her pride would not let her accept their help. Besides, it would not be fair to her children—they would need a father as much as they needed a mother.

Blinking back a tear, she brushed a light kiss on each girl's cheek and then tiptoed from the room. She was still young—there was no need to despair of having a family of her own just yet. Her weariness combined with the sherry must be making her maudlin.

"Where have you been?" The accusatory male voice hit her the moment she entered her own room.

Put off balance by the sudden and unexpected attack, she stopped short and blinked disbelievingly at the dark man lounging on her bed. "I was checking on the girls." What on earth was Khair Bey doing in the servants' quarters—in her room? Shouldn't he be down in the parlor listening to Mrs.

Tofts tinkling away on the pianoforte, and ogling her half-exposed breasts?

"It doesn't take more than an hour to check on a pair of children." His voice was a harsh sneer of accusation. "Have you been with another man? Your lover, perhaps?"

She bit back an amused snort. Now that her brain had recovered from the shock of being confronted by a man in her bedroom, she began to see the absurdity of the situation. He had intruded into her private quarters and then had the audacity to question where she had been. "Oh, for heaven's sake," she retorted. "Don't be ridiculous. If you must know, I was having a nightcap with Mrs. Botham in her living room. I spend most of my evenings in her company."

His face grew fractionally less furious. "And just who is this Mrs. Botham?"

"She is the housekeeper here, and a most respectable woman. Besides, what I do in my free time is none of your business and you certainly have no right to quiz me about it." She held the door open and stared him in the eye. "Now, if you have finished interrogating me about my private life, I think you had better leave."

He did not move from the bed. "I'm afraid I do not agree with you."

"I beg your pardon?" She injected her voice with pure ice. How dare he lie down on her bed and refuse to move? This was a civilized country and it followed the rule of law. Guest of the household or not, he had no right to be in her bedroom, not after she had asked him to leave. Of course, a real gentleman would never have entered it without her express invitation in the first place. She'd known that he would bear watching, and he'd proved he was not to be trusted.

"I have no intention of leaving. Now, shut the door, will you? You are letting in a draft."

Just who did he think he was? She would not be ordered about by some foreign potentate at his whim, and be expected to obey as if she were a slave. "Out," she ordered, "or I will summon the footmen and have you thrown out." It was a disappointment that he was just like all the other men who tried to get too familiar with her. Worse, indeed, since he had the temerity to invade her bedchamber in her absence and make himself quite at home there. None of her other suitors had been quite so determined.

He merely laughed at her fury. "That would not be a wise move. I am a guest in the household, here at the behest of Mr. Winterbottom. It would be a brave footman, or a foolish one, who would lay violent hands on an invited guest for one little complaint from a nursery maid."

"Mr. Winterbottom will ask you to leave if I tell him how you have insulted me." She looked wistfully at Khair Bey as he lay on her bed. How nice it would be if a gentleman was interested in talking to her for once, instead of merely being intent on taking off her clothes at the earliest opportunity. She had a heart and a soul. Clearly, this Khair Bey was not the sort of man who cared about her inner self. It was a pity, for he was a good deal more handsome than any of the other men who had shown a disreputable interest in her.

"I think not. He wants to do business with me rather badly. It will be greatly to his profit, and, incidentally, to mine as well." He spread his hands wide. "And what is this great insult you have accused me of? I wish nothing but to talk to you where we cannot be overheard. Is such a wish to be construed as an insult? For truthfully, I do not see how I could have offended you otherwise."

She frowned at him, the sherry still addling her wits a trifle. Clearly he could be as charming as the snake in the Garden of Eden when he chose to be. And just as slippery. She did not trust him an inch, nor did she believe he wanted nothing more than to talk to her. He was young and virile enough to want more than words. "You offend me simply by being here. It shows that you have no respect for me, or you would leave at my request." Whatever he might assume about her, she was not his for the taking. He was not the first—and undoubtedly not the last—to think her easy prey.

"Come now, close the door. Or do you intend for every person passing by to see that you are entertaining me in your bedroom?"

She stamped her foot on the floor, heedless of the noise her shoe made on the wooden boards. "I am not entertaining you. I am asking you to leave." She had never before met someone so infuriating, so able to twist events to suit his own purposes.

"I'm not sure that the distinction will be evident to everyone in the house. But, of course, if you have no objection to being thought a woman of easy virtue, then please, leave the door open. That way, passersby will be able to form their own opinions."

Annoyingly, he was right. As it was, she was lucky that no one had happened by to hear them quarreling and to bear tales against her to her employers. If she were to get a reputation for entertaining gentlemen in her private quarters, however unwillingly, the Winterbottoms would certainly ask her to leave and refuse to provide her with a reference. If the gossip about her got out, as it was bound to do, she would never find another post as a nursery maid. No decent family would want a woman of questionable reputation bringing up their daughters.

Heaving a sigh of irritation with the situation he had forced her into, she shut the door quietly but firmly behind her. "There, it is shut. Now, say what you have to say to me, and please leave."

He patted the bed beside him. "Come and sit down. You look tired."

She *was* tired. Her head was swimming with a combination of fatigue and alcohol. All she wanted to do was crawl under her bedcovers, blow out the candle, and drift off to sleep—alone. "You are in my way."

His smile was a gleam of white in the deep gloom of evening. "I don't bite."

Her legs seemed reluctant to hold her upright any longer. She briefly considered collapsing onto the floor, but it was cold, hard, and uninviting, not to mention that it would be terribly undignified. "I'm not in the mood to play games with you," she muttered, sitting gingerly on the bed, as far away from him as she could manage, and laying her head back on the pillows. "Please, go away."

"Not until I have what I came for."

Her eyes had drifted shut, but at his words, she snapped them open again and propped herself up on her elbows. "I told you, I am not in the mood to play games," she said tartly. "I have no desire to become your mistress. I am perfectly happy as a nursery maid. I do not need nor do I want a wealthy lover to buy me extravagant presents. I do not find you in the least bit attractive and I am not open to persuasion. The footmen from down the hall will come running if you try to use force. In short, you are wasting your time with me." Her little outburst over, she closed her eyes and rested back on the pillows again.

"Time spent with a pretty woman is never a waste."

She sniffed at his persistence. "Even if the woman in question would rather be sleeping?"

"Are you trying to drive me away with your insults?"

"Just with my honesty." A deep yawn added conviction to her words.

He heaved a sigh. "I can see it is too late in the day to have a sensible conversation with you. Come, give me a kiss and send me on my way."

She opened one eye and looked at him suspiciously. "You will leave me in peace if I kiss you? Now, why don't I believe you?"

"Because you are far too cynical for one as young and as pretty as you are."

"If I were old and ugly, there would be less need for me to be cynical about men's motives," she muttered. Surely he did not think he was the only man who had tried to corner her and steal a kiss.

"I swear it. One kiss and I will leave you here alone in your cold, narrow bed."

"Do you swear it on the Bible?"

"I swear it on the grave of my ancestors."

He sounded serious enough. And the footmen were only just down the hall. Whatever Khair Bey might think, they would come to her rescue if he got out of hand. Ollie was as big as a bear while Jem was well-known for his hasty temper, and neither of them took kindly to visitors who overstepped the bounds of courtesy. If she were to call for them, they would eject her unwanted guest before he knew what hit him.

But for the first time in her life she *wanted* to be kissed. She wanted to feel the pressure of his mouth on hers, and the scrape of his stubbled chin against her face. Would he taste of tobacco and port wine like the other men who had tried to kiss her or of something altogether different—spicier and more exotic than she had ever dreamed of? Would his mouth be as soft and gentle as it looked, or hard and demanding? "Come, kiss me then," she murmured, as much to herself as to him.

"You are inviting me to kiss you?"

"It is clearly the fastest way to get you to leave me alone." She would admit to nothing more. Certainly she would not let him see how very much she wanted to be kissed by him. That would be tantamount to begging him to take advantage of her. She had not drunk enough sherry to do something quite that foolish.

With her eyes shut, she felt him move over her, his bulky form blocking out the dim candlelight.

His mouth was a gentle pressure on hers, brushing her lips with a softness she would never have believed possible. His touch was as light as a feather, and just as insubstantial. She swallowed a moan of protest and lifted her head off the pillows toward him, seeking a deeper contact.

For the first time in her life, she had agreed to be kissed—*asked* to be kissed. He ought at least to make it worth her while, instead of brushing her lips with his as if he were made of gossamer instead of flesh and blood. What had she done to make him lose interest, to repel him? His lack of ardor was almost insulting.

As if he were reading her thoughts, he met her mouth with his, gently pushing her back onto the pillows, deepening the kiss as she desired. His lips pressed against hers with barely suppressed passion. This time he let her feel how much he was holding back, how great his desire for her was, and how carefully he was keeping it caged.

She did not want his desire trammeled. She wanted to see it let loose, to have it run wild and free, and to meet it with her own. His skin smelled faintly of sandalwood and of something else, something earthy and male. She nuzzled into his neck, trying to capture the elusive smell, to categorize it. The scent was nothing she recognized, but it called to her blood. Heaven help her, she wanted this man. She wanted him as she had never wanted any other. The kiss he had given her merely whetted her appetite for his touch. If she did not get more of the taste of him, she would run mad with need.

Though her head told her what a bad idea it was to encourage this man to further intimacies, her body was screaming at her to continue, to go further with him than she ever had before. Her private parts were tingling with the desire to get closer to him, to press herself up against him and feel the touch of his skin on hers. The clamor from her body was so loud and insistent that it drowned out any words of warning—all sense of caution was lost in the upwelling of her own desire.

His mouth opened on hers, and she opened hers in response, as if it were the most natural thing in the world. His tongue caressed hers, stroking her to a fever pitch.

He tasted of sherry—or perhaps she tasted herself on his tongue. No, it wasn't sherry but something more exotic. She could not put a name to the taste, but whatever it was, she craved more of it.

The deeper he kissed her, the more she wanted him to continue. The tingling grew stronger between her thighs, where she could feel herself growing both hot and moist. If she touched herself now, she would be dripping wet. This awareness of her body was a new sensation—the very knowledge of her needs making them more insistent.

Her hands crept up to rest on his shoulders, pulling him toward her. She wanted more than the touch of his mouth on hers—she wanted to feel his body stretched out against her own, pressing into her.

At her unspoken invitation to get closer, he swung his legs up onto the bed and stretched out next to her on the coverlet.

She sighed with pleasure as she snuggled up next to him, the warmth of his body spreading through hers to pool down low in her belly. Her breasts peaked to hard tips, and she rubbed them against his chest, abrading them on the rough fabric of her chemise. She had not expected them to be so sensitive, and the contact made a shiver travel through her entire body.

Khair Bey drew back from her kiss. "Are you cold?"

She moaned with protest at his withdrawal and pulled him back down toward her. "Maybe just a little. Come closer and keep me warm."

Truthfully, even though the night had fallen and she had no

fire in her room, she was far from cold. She was so hot she was practically burning up, as if a particularly virulent fever had her in its grip. She desired him with a craving so strong that it was like a disease, robbing her of the ability to think of anything but her need for him.

He moved closer to her, his body cradling her in its heat. She pressed against him, her breasts against his chest, her belly against his belly, and her thighs against his. He settled between her legs as if he was made to fit her, and she opened her thighs to make room for him where he needed it most.

Her face flamed in the darkness to acknowledge the length of his hardened shaft pressing between her legs. She wriggled against him until he was positioned right where she wanted him to be, with his shaft nudging at the entrance to her parts. Only the thin wool of his trousers, and the even thinner layers of cotton and serge of her shift and gown, served as a fragile barrier that kept them from meeting skin on skin.

He was hard against her softness, dark where she was pale, the perfect foil to her femininity. The sherry she had drunk made her bold and she pressed up against him, feeling the hardness of him tantalizing her.

She felt his hands creep under her gown, stroking her legs through her stockings. Then, he untied her garters and drew her stockings down over her legs, removing them and her slippers at once.

His hands burned a path back up her calves, over her knees, and then along her thighs.

In the back of her head, alarm bells were ringing, and she clamped her thighs tightly together so he could not touch her just where she longed to be touched most of all.

He did not force the issue, but took his hands out from under her skirts.

Her mixture of disappointment and relief was short-lived, for he ran his hands instead over her breasts, then stopped at her buttons. "Don't," she protested weakly as he wriggled the buttons free one by one. He took no notice of her whispered refusal, not stopping until her bodice was quite undone.

Nothing protected her breasts now but the thin cotton of her chemise. It was no barrier to his hands. He found the tie that kept it fastened at the top and pulled the strings undone. Her bodice was pushed quite off her shoulders and her chemise had been pulled down to her waist before she realized what he was doing.

By the time she understood what he was up to, she had lost the desire to stop him. He was kneading her naked breasts with his hands. When he brushed her supersensitive nipples with the tips of his fingers, the sensation made her gasp and arch her back off the bed. When he leaned over her and took one of her nipples in his mouth, she felt as though she had died and gone to heaven. His tongue teased her breasts one after the other, making her nipples stand up hard and cold in the evening air.

This time, when he snaked his hand under her skirts again,

her thighs were no longer pressed tightly together, but had relaxed with pleasure. His fingers crept up to tangle in the nest of curls at the top of her thighs, and to dip between her legs and stroke her most private parts.

"Do you want me to leave you now?" he whispered.

"You ought to go," she said, as she writhed against his fingers. "You should not be touching me like this."

"Tell me to leave and I will go," he promised, slipping the tip of his finger into her wetness. "Tell me to leave, and really mean it."

How could she tell him to leave when she was drunk on his touch—when every particle of her being was yearning for him? "Please." She wasn't sure if she was begging him to leave her or to continue tormenting her.

"Please what?" he demanded. He moved his finger slowly in and out of her, sinking a little deeper with each thrust. Her pussy tightened around him, not wanting to let him go. "If you want me to leave, you have to tell me so."

She could not force the words out. Not when she wanted him to stay so badly. "I can't."

He took her hand in his and moved it onto his trousers where his shaft pressed firmly against the fabric. "Touch me like I am touching you."

"I can't," she repeated, but her hands had other ideas. Almost of their own volition, they fumbled with the buttons on his trousers, freeing him to stand up proudly. She stroked it with a growing sense of wonderment, feeling the hard length of him under her fingers. "I have never touched a man like this before."

He groaned with pleasure at her touch. "Don't stop."

What would it feel like to have this inside her instead of his fingers? If a single finger made her feel so full, what would this do to her? She caressed him harder at the thought, and his fingers thrust in and out of her faster than before. Though she would never let him ruin her, she still could dream.

Just when she thought she was about to fly to pieces in his arms, he took his fingers away. "Do you want me to leave you now?"

She tightened her grip on him, stroking him hard and fast. "No. Don't go." She didn't care what anyone else thought—she wanted him to remain with her. She wanted his fingers back inside her, showing her the way to heaven.

"If I stay, I will make love to you. I will make you mine. Do you want me to do that?"

"You will take my virginity?" The thought was like a bucket of cold water thrown over her head. Her grasp on him slackened. She wriggled away from him and pressed up against the wall. To allow him to put his fingers inside her was one thing, but to take his cock was another matter. As much as she wanted to feel him inside her, she had never intended to allow him that ultimate liberty. She had not realized she had gone so far—that she was so close to losing herself. It was the sherry, damn it all! She would never touch the stuff again.

"You are a maiden?"

She nodded quietly in the darkness, suddenly ashamed of her wantonness. No man would believe that she was a virgin if she behaved like this in his arms. She was no better than the men who pursued her—and she had a lot more to lose than they did. "I am." She still burned for him as before, but her head was starting to clear. She shuddered at the foolish risk she had taken. "Please, I do not want you to ruin me."

With a muttered curse, he rolled away from her and fumbled with his buttons. "I had better leave you now, then."

"Yes, please go." This time, despite the burning in her blood and the wetness between her thighs, she really meant it.

Khair Bey made his way back to his own room on feet as soft and noiseless as a cat's.

He wasn't sure exactly what had made him stop consummating the seduction of the pretty nursery maid tonight. In spite of her feeble protests, she had clearly been willing enough and she had enjoyed his attentions. Her pussy was drenched with wetness and she had moved against his hand as if she were drunk on pleasure. She was so wet and ready that not even her virginity would have proved much of a barrier. He could have slid his engorged cock into her without the least resistance, not stopping until he was buried in her up to the hilt. He could have fucked her then, with long, slow strokes, until her pussy convulsed around him, milking him of every drop of semen in his body as he came inside her.

In her current state of inebriation, she would not even have realized what he had done until it was too late. Her virginity would have been long gone before she even woke up to the fact.

Maybe that was what had stopped him—the thought that she had taken too much drink to fully realize what she was doing. When he took a woman, he demanded that all her senses be engaged and totally focused on their lovemaking. Seducing women who did not know what they were doing had never been his style. Taking a virgin in such a thoughtless way, however eager she appeared to be at the time, would not sit well with his conscience.

Not that it helped him in his current predicament. He'd been horny as hell all evening, and only the promise he'd made to himself of filling Louisa's pussy with his come had kept his libido in check. He was paying the price for his dalliance now, with a cock so hard and swollen it felt monstrous. It was too late to arrange an assignation with another woman, even if he had been able to get the thought of Louisa out of his head. But he didn't want another woman—he wanted her. Now that he faced the reality of a cold bed on his own instead of sharing hers, his balls ached with unfulfilled desire.

He shut the door to his room behind him and pulled off his evening clothes with careless haste and tossed them on the floor. His valet could see to them in the morning.

With nothing to confine it, his throbbing cock waved bravely even in the cold, night air. He flung himself down on the bed, stroking himself and feeling the taut, stretched skin under his hand. He felt both thicker and longer than usual—the effect of Louisa's touch. He should've let her stroke him into fulfilment, and then at least he would've received some pleasure from the evening's debacle. Damn it, he'd never get to sleep in this state.

He lounged naked on his bed, continuing to stroke himself with one hand. His own hand didn't feel as soft as Louisa's, but it would have to do.

He leaned back on the pillows and shut his eyes, imagining that Louisa's hands were on him, stroking his body, playing with his nipples. He reached up to caress his chest, thinking how it would feel to have her naked beside him, and as ready for him as he was for her. He would take those luscious breasts of hers into his mouth and lower her onto his cock until he filled her completely. Then she would ride him up and down, her head thrown back and her back arched to thrust her breasts into his hands.

Up and down she would ride him, his shaft getting deeper and harder with every thrust. His cock was straining and his balls got tight and hard as he stroked himself faster. His breath was coming short and he knew he was going to come. She would ride on him to her own orgasm. Then, as she sucked him dry, he would thrust into her once, twice, three times, until he came continuously with the force of a river in flood.

His seed erupted from his body, spraying over his naked chest. There it stuck, rapidly congealing as it cooled.

He gave his balls one last loving stroke and then rolled over and under the covers, grimacing at the way the sheets stuck to him. He still badly wanted to fuck Louisa, but his need had been tamed to a manageable state. He would see the girl again tomorrow, and the day after, and he would not be so lenient the next time he had her alone in the dark.

Three

The following morning, Louisa was playing croquet in the garden with Hester and Prudence when Khair Bey found her again. She had just stooped down to retie Hester's shoelace when she saw him striding toward them. "That's better," she said to Hester, as she tied the laces in a double knot before hurriedly getting to her feet again and brushing down her gown. Her face was hot, and her flush was from more than the already warm morning sun. Khair Bey seemed to have the knack of catching her at a disadvantage—if she wasn't tipsy with sherry, she was on her knees on the dusty grass, attending to a child. "Now you won't trip when you run after your ball."

Khair Bey was the last person she wanted to see this morning after her naughty frolic with him last night. She could not look him in the eye, but kept her eyes fixed firmly on her shoes.

"Miss Clemens." His voice had a magnetic quality to it. She could not help but be drawn to it, even though she knew she ought to run away from everything he represented. Last night had proven only too clearly the danger he posed to her. He was bad news.

"Khair Bey." Her own voice was cool and impersonal—far more so than she was feeling. In the bright glare of the morning, her behavior the night before filled her with shame. How could she have behaved so wantonly with a man she had only just met? He would think she was his for the taking, nothing more than a pretty servant girl to while away his free hours with during his stay in Naples. It would be a meaningless interlude for him, but one that spelled potential ruin and disaster for her.

Single men were expected to sow their wild oats, but single young women were not supposed to have such inclinations. For the first time, the unfairness of it rankled with her.

The sobering truth was that last night she *had* been his for the taking. For some reason, he had not pressed home his advantage, and for that she was truly thankful. But his forbearance did not lessen her shame. It was not due to her good sense or her self-control that she still possessed her virginity today.

She turned her head away from him to hide her embarrassment. Whatever he was hoping for, there would be no repeat of last night. She did not trust herself to get anywhere near him. He brought out the worst in her. Even just the sight of him this morning had already made her nipples as hard as stone and set her parts tingling all over again. Just one look from him and she felt hot with desire.

Besides, after drinking too much the night before and then sleeping badly, she felt tired and heavy. It had been a real effort to drag herself out of her bed this morning. She had no strength to fight him off.

"And Prudence and Hester, too. How delightful." He gave the girls a courtly bow and they giggled with delight as they dipped him a little curtsy. "What are you doing out here in the garden so early in the morning?"

Prudence held up her croquet mallet as if it were a trophy. "We are playing croquet and I am winning. See, that's where my ball is." She pointed to her yellow ball, which she had already hit through three hoops. "I am always yellow. It's my lucky color."

Hester made a face. "I'm nearly caught up with you. And besides, it's my turn now. And I bet *he* could beat you." She took him by the hand and tugged him over to the heap of unused mallets and balls by the start. "Come and play with us. Prudence always wins and it's getting boring. I bet *you* could beat her if you tried."

"Don't bother Khair Bey, sweetheart." Louisa handed Hester back her mallet in an effort to distract her. "I am sure he has lots of important business to do. He is too busy to play with us." She hoped that he would take the hint and leave them to finish their game in peace.

He did no such thing. Shooting her a sideways glance of amusement at her blatant attempt to be rid of him, he picked Hester up under her arms and swung her high in the air. She squealed with delight. "I would love to play croquet with you and your sister," he said, as he swung the still-squealing girl back down onto the grass, "if Miss Clements doesn't mind."

"She doesn't mind at all, do you?" Prudence cajoled Louisa solemnly, holding out her arms to be picked up and swung, too. "Louisa, please tell the man he is allowed to come and play with us."

"I don't know what your mother would think," Louisa temporized, searching for a suitable excuse to send him packing. Could she survive the rest of the morning in his company? She already knew how dangerous he was to her sense of self-preservation. A whole morning of being close to him, talking and laughing, with him brushing up against her accidentally as they fought over a croquet ball would torment her—knowing how ready he was to be close to her and yet having to keep him at a distance. She still could not bear to look him in the eye.

"Mrs. Winterbottom herself told me where I could find you this morning, so I'm sure she would have no objection to me joining in the fun." His eyes gleamed with triumph at having so neatly overruled any objections she might make to his company. "Hester and Prudence are well chaperoned by their nursemaid, so there can be no impropriety there."

Hester and Prudence both went into fits of pleased giggles at the suggestion they were old enough to need a chaperone.

Louisa bowed gracefully to the inevitable. "Pick yourself a mallet, sir, and come and join in the game. I have to warn you, though," she added ingenuously, "we play strictly by the rules. We do not tolerate cheats, do we girls?"

Hester and Prudence giggled harder than ever. "No cheating," they agreed.

"And do not expect any favors because you are a latecomer to the game," she warned him. "You will have to start at the beginning, just as we did."

Khair Bey raised an eyebrow at her commands, but picked up the green mallet meekly enough and dribbled the matching ball up to the starting line. The three of them watched as he gave his mallet a few practice swings and then lined himself up for the first shot.

Louisa winked at Prudence and she nodded back in secret agreement.

Just as he swung the mallet, Prudence gave a sudden shriek of terror. Startled by the noise, he whirled around, hitting the ball off course and into a patch of long grass under the tree. "Are you hurt?"

Prudence looked at him, wide-eyed and innocent. "I saw a bee. It has gone now."

"Are you sure it didn't sting you?" A look of concern lingered on his face.

"Yes, I'm sure. It flew away." She waved him away with one hand, and went back to studying the croquet green.

Mallet in hand, Hester skipped up to her ball. "My turn now." Her tongue stuck out over her top lip in concentration and she smacked her ball smartly, hitting Prudence's neatly out of the way and, incidentally, clearing the way for Louisa's.

"Ooh, good shot," Louisa said, tapping her own ball through the next hoop. When it came to playing croquet with the girls, she had to be as cutthroat as they were or they would leave her for dead. No quarter, no mercy were the rules they played by. Tired as she was, a good game of croquet always managed to raise her spirits.

Khair Bey strolled over to the tree and tapped his own ball back onto the green. The two girls exchanged identical looks of triumph. One little scream and they had made him waste two shots.

His luck didn't get any better as the morning wore on. The girls ignored him for a few rounds, concentrating on eliminating their most serious opponents—each other—until it looked as though he might have an outside chance of catching up with them. Then Prudence saw another bee, and Hester accidentally knocked against him just when he was taking a shot. Even Louisa couldn't resist the temptation to knock his ball away from the next hoop with a well-timed hit of her own.

Not until Prudence saw a third bee did Khair Bey turn on them all suspiciously. "No cheating?" he asked, a disbelieving tone in his voice. "You play fair?"

Prudence gave an easy shrug, quite unconcerned at the unspoken accusation. "I don't like bees. I can't help it if they live in the garden."

"Louisa is always telling me how clumsy I am," Hester explained, very seriously. "She says I need to learn how to walk like a lady."

"It is perfectly within the rules to knock away your opponents' balls if you can," Louisa added for good measure.

"I see." He spoke with a certain finality, as if he surely did see. "You are a trio of nefarious double-dealers and I shall have to watch my back, not to mention my croquet ball."

"What does 'nefarious' mean?" Hester asked, accidentally tripping again and coincidentally knocking Khair Bey's ball into a slightly less favorable position. He watched the whole charade with a wry smile of amusement, but he didn't voice a word of complaint.

"In this context, it means 'smarter and sneakier than I am,'" Louisa said with a grin. Really, she ought not to encourage such positively piratical tendencies in her charges, but it was such fun. No dully polite lawn games for the three of them, but a battle that called for sharp wits, even sharper eyes, and utterly ruthless tactics. The knowledge that Mrs. Winterbottom was sure to strenuously disapprove of such unladylike behavior just made it all the more exciting.

"Now that," he said with a mischievous glint in his eyes, "is a challenge that I absolutely cannot resist."

From then on, the game took on a whole new flavor. Khair Bey proved to be as clever and sneaky as the rest of them at sabotage and fighting dirty. Not only did he prove adept at knocking other people's croquet balls far away from the action, but he quickly learned the other unsavory tactics employed by his opponents. Hay fever, he claimed, was responsible for the loud sneeze that startled Hester and put her off her shot. He really had not meant to bump into Prudence at a crucial moment, and as for her claim that he had nudged her ball away from the hoop with the tip of his boot, why, that was simply preposterous. Did the girls think so badly of him that they thought he could behave in such an unsportsmanlike manner?

But it was Louisa who suffered most from his presence. He had a different way altogether of putting her off her game. How could she concentrate on hitting her croquet ball when he was leaning over her shoulder, his breath burning her neck with its heat? He took every opportunity to bump into her, to brush against her with his body when the girls were looking away, and to offer her sly caresses under the guise of helping her hold her mallet, until she was a mass of screaming nerves.

She wanted to forget that last night had ever happened, that she had behaved so shamelessly in the arms of a stranger. But every heated look he gave her, every touch of his body against hers, innocent though it may be, reminded her of what she most wanted to forget. Their closeness made her remember how badly her body had craved his, how she had nearly melted with the force of her passion.

Though she fought against her baser desires, she could feel them growing, threatening to overwhelm her as they had the night before. She wanted him to touch her again. She craved for him to strip her naked and touch her everywhere, to ease the burning inside her. Thank heaven they were in the garden, for if he was lying next to her right now in the privacy of her room, she was desperate enough to let him do anything he wanted to her—even take her virginity—as long as he assuaged her terrible need for him.

She turned around to inspect the layout of the game. He was closer to her than she expected, and she accidentally brushed the front of his trousers with the back of her hand. She could not help lingering there for just a second or two, remembering how hard he had been, what it had been like to hold him in her hand, to have him in her power. It was hell to be so close to him and yet so far away.

His grin told her that he had noticed her lingering, hesitant caress.

At long last, Prudence whacked her ball through the last hoop, and Louisa dissolved into a long-suppressed, almost hysterical sigh of relief. Finally she could take the girls back inside for luncheon, and escape his tormenting presence. Khair Bey could not follow them into the nursery. She would have some much-needed peace to regain her equilibrium and to marshal her badly weakened defenses.

Prudence was exultant. "I won, I won!" she crowed, jumping up and down with triumph.

Hester made a face. "You always win, but this time you almost didn't. Khair Bey almost beat you."

"He did not." Prudence was not going to be robbed of her moment of glory. "He was miles and miles behind." Her voice dripped with disdain.

"He did, too." Then Hester's face brightened. "It was fun playing with him. Did you see his face when you pretended to see a bee?"

"I *did* see a bee," Prudence protested weakly.

"Come, girls, tidy away the croquet things. It is nearly time for luncheon, and your mama has promised to take you to town this afternoon to order you some new slippers."

At the reminder of this treat, the girls hurried off to do her bidding.

Louisa shot a glance at Khair Bey. How could she want someone so badly when she knew he was not good for her? One idle touch from him and she forgot all about what she really wanted out of life—children of her own, and a husband to help raise them. Being a wealthy man's mistress was not the way to achieve her dreams. True, he might give her children, but they would live the lives of outcasts, with a mother who could never be a part of respectable society. However tempted she was by him, however much she wanted to spread her legs wide for him and beg him to take her, she had to hold on to that thought. Giving in to his seduction would bring her only a fleeting pleasure, but would carry with it a lasting regret. "You are the most dreadful cheat I have ever met."

"I have learned from the experts," he said, gesturing at Hester and Prudence, who were squabbling amicably enough as they gathered up the hoops from the lawn.

"They arc only children."

He was silent for a few moments, simply looking at her face

as if he wanted to memorize every plane and hollow. "Meet me here this afternoon, in the garden."

His request showed how little he knew about life as a servant. Clearly he had never been at another person's beck and call to earn his bread. "I can't. Unlike you, I am not a guest here. I have work to do." She tried to keep a note of envy from creeping into her voice. Oh, how she would love to have an afternoon to while away at her ease in the sun, without endless chores to keep her busy. To lie on the grass in the garden and feel the sun beat down on the back of her head, and to know that she could linger there all afternoon if she pleased. But servants, even nursery maids, did not often have the luxury of rest.

"Even while the girls are out shopping with their mother?"

"My duties do not stop at looking after the girls. I have to keep their room clean and tidy, and mend their clothes and stockings. I am terribly behind on the mending." Her voice sounded weak, even to herself. She was surprised by how much she wanted to escape her duties for an hour or two.

"Come for a walk with me instead. Just a short walk around the garden."

"You have been playing with the girls all morning, and now you want to go walking in the afternoon?" He was a businessman, not a man of leisure with time to burn. "Did you not come to Naples to look after your business?"

"It is nothing that cannot wait."

"And if I refuse to walk with you?"

"Then I shall seek you out in the nursery and sit with you while you do your mending." A wolfish look came into his eyes. "On second thought, perhaps I would prefer to meet you in the nursery than in the garden. With the girls away, it will be quite deserted. I shall have you entirely to myself."

"I will meet you in the garden," she said hurriedly. She could not risk having him alone with her in a deserted part of the house. She wanted him so badly she did not trust herself—or him, for that matter. The garden was much more public and therefore safer. "If I can."

Maybe the housekeeper would have some errands for her to run, or need some help putting up preserves for the winter. That would keep her safely occupied and out of harm's way for the afternoon and give her an excuse not to meet with him.

"I will be waiting for you."

Khair Bey excused himself from the luncheon table as soon as was polite, and strolled out into the garden. Thankfully for the sake of his patience, Mrs. Winterbottom was anxious to take her daughters on their promised jaunt to town, and did not linger over the midday meal. Mr. Winterbottom had excused himself shortly after breakfast to take care of some business at one of his warehouses.

Sheltered from the breeze, the garden was baking in the summer heat. He lifted his face to the sky, enjoying the sun's warm caress. In Italy the sun lacked the fierce heat of a Moroccan summer's day, when even the sun-loving lizards sought out a shady spot to sleep away the day.

He wasn't sure whether or not he wanted Louisa to seek him out in the garden. If she did, he would be glad that she wanted to spend some time with him, but if she did not, it would give him an excuse to go and find her in the deserted nursery. If she put up no more resistance than she had last night, he would have the opportunity to take her twice before her charges came back from their shopping expedition—first a quick one to take the edge off his need, and then a long, slow, exploratory fuck as he learned what she liked the most, and as he taught her how to please him best in return.

He made a slight adjustment to his trousers. He could see her right now, stepping out of her gown in the dappled sunshine of the early afternoon, pulling her shift over her head, and standing proudly naked in front of him, her nipples peaked to tightness. He would kneel in front of her, lick her pussy, and tease her with his fingers until she was trembling with desire for him and on the brink of an orgasm. Only then would he position her the way he wanted to take her first. Imagining her bent naked over the back of one of the nursery chairs—her legs apart and her pussy wet and open for him, wordlessly pleading for him to take her—was having the expected effect on him.

He strode around the garden with growing impatience as he waited. The carriage rolled out into the street and Hester— or was it Prudence?—waved at him as it drove away, but still Louisa did not appear.

He'd awakened ready for her this morning, his cock standing stiffly to attention, and he'd been in much the same state ever since. Taking her straight to his bed for an urgent tumble was looking more attractive with every minute that passed.

He paced up and down the garden path, barely seeing the summer flowers blooming in the beds beside him. If she refused to come to him, he would go to her as he had promised. She had led him on for long enough and he had been more than easy on her, stopping their dalliance before taking her virginity. If she thought he would continue to be so restrained in the face of her provocation, she was mistaken. He had no patience left for her teasing.

Just as he had despaired of her coming to meet him and was making his way back inside to find her in the nursery, she came running out of the house, her bonnet dangling from one hand. "I could not get away," she said, when she had caught her breath. "Mrs. Botham needed some help in the kitchen, and since the girls were away, I could not refuse."

He did not believe a word of her hurried excuses. She had kept him waiting for as long as she dared, and then came out to meet him so that he would not look for her and create a scandal in the servants' quarters. Even though she clearly wanted him, she was fighting her seduction in every little way she could.

If she wanted him to chase her, then he would oblige—for a while.

She could only delay the inevitable, not escape it. Sooner or later she would be his, and all her small subterfuges, all her attempts to hide from his pursuit of her, would be over.

"Come, walk with me." He held out his arm. Though she bit at her bottom lip with worry, she took his arm and fell into step beside him.

At the rear of the house, the garden rose in a set of terraces, with a grove of lemon trees on the lower slopes giving way to a stand of cypress trees farther up. With one accord, they strolled through the citrus orchard and made their way toward the cypress trees, which were farther away from the house and offered more shade and a good measure of privacy from prying eyes. The fewer witnesses there were to his courtship of Louisa, the more easily she would succumb to his lure. There was less virtue in resisting temptation if there was no audience to applaud your efforts.

Once they reached the line of cypress trees, they paused and looked back down at the house. From this distance it looked like a summerhouse, set back from the road and surrounded by gardens; the sort of house a man might give to his mistress—a house built for pleasure.

Khair Bey could imagine installing Louisa in such a place—a house full of sunshine, laughter, and love—and children, *his* children. The thought brought a smile to his face. Louisa would be a good mother.

He wasn't sure exactly when the idea of taking Louisa back to Morocco with him and quietly installing her in one of his houses had taken root. Maybe it was after she had turned down his advances in her bedroom, pleading for her virginity. Or perhaps it was after he had awakened this morning with a stiff cock and an urgent need to fuck her—and only her.

Whenever the idea had first come to him, it was now a settled plan in his mind. His larger house in the town of Medina would be suitable, where he could visit her without raising eyebrows among the more conservative members of his community.

He could never take her back to his casbah in the Rif Mountains and flaunt his mistress under the noses of his people, his family, and his own mother. In Medina he would be just another businessman, and possessed an anonymity he could never have in the smaller community of his real home. As soon as he could make the necessary arrangements, Medina would be her new home.

He knew instinctively that one night with her would not be enough. He had been fooling himself if he thought that would do more than build his appetite. He would want to keep her for years, if not forever. She was more innocent, more vulnerable than his usual lovers. He generally took up with married women who knew exactly what he offered them—a night's pleasure in exchange for a pretty bauble in the morning. They were easy, uncomplicated amours.

She was a virgin still—though if he had his way, she would not remain so for long. In exchange for her maidenhead, he would make her his pampered mistress, providing her with a lifetime of luxury in return for taking him to her bed. It seemed a fair enough exchange.

If he ever decided to give in to his mother's wishes and take a wife, he would ensure that she—and any children she might have—remained well provided for. Once she gave herself over to his keeping, he would honor his pledge to protect her until he died, and even then he would be sure to provide for her in his will.

Such generous offers did not come the way of simple nurse-maids very often, even ones as charming as Louisa. She would be a fool to turn down the material benefits he could offer her to remain faithful to him.

Next to him, Louisa gave a sigh. "It is a lovely view from up here." There was a thread of melancholy in her voice.

"And yet it makes you sad?"

"Only the thought of leaving it."

"You are thinking of leaving soon?" Had she already guessed the plan he had in store for her? Would she try to increase the price she demanded from him? The thought did not please him—he did not like greedy, grasping women.

"I will have to one day. When the children grow."

"You will like Morocco. It looks a little like this, only it is drier. Wilder, less tamed."

At his description of his home, she threw off the melancholy that was clouding her mood. "What is it like in Morocco?" she asked brightly. "Mrs. Botham said that you all have fifty wives apiece, and that you keep your women locked away and never let them see the sun."

Her précis of Moroccan society made him laugh out loud. "Mrs. Botham is an expert on such matters?"

Louisa's bottom lip dropped. "How am I to know? I have never been there."

"Neither has Mrs. Botham, I'll wager."

"You are the first Moorish man I have ever seen. So, do you have fifty wives?"

"Not me."

"How many wives do you have, then?"

"None at all."

She was silent for a moment. "Concubines, then?" she asked, her face pink with the intimacy of the question. "How many of *them* do you have? And do you keep them all locked away?"

Her face was so earnest that he could not forgo teasing her. "You have guessed my secret," he admitted, his face straight. "I have at least fifty concubines, or maybe more. It has been so long since I last counted."

She nibbled on her lower lip, looking quite delightfully confused at the idea. "And do they all live with you in a harem?"

Her question made him smile. The truth was so much less glamorous. Though men would always be men, openly taking concubines was frowned upon in the Berber community from which he came, as was the practice of *nikah mut'a*, or taking a temporary wife.

Though Arabic law allowed the taking of four permanent wives and any number of temporary ones, Berbers had largely ignored the Arabic customs and remained loyal to their own.

Family was important to his people, and to him. The villagers who lived in the Rif believed in one husband, one wife. Taking a second wife could make a man an outcast in the Berber community, even though it was legal under Arabic law.

He would have to be careful not to flaunt Louisa as his property, and to keep her well hidden. As bey, he was expected to set an example for his people and not to fill his houses with women of loose morals. The days of the sultan with a vast and varied harem of wives and concubines from all over the country was long gone. Even the sultan was expected to show moderation in his desires.

Still, the women's quarters of his casbah would count as a harem, he supposed. His mother and her sisters lived there with a handful of maids apiece. He also sheltered the occasional great aunt or cousin, or other female relative who needed a home. His mother was in charge—he did not interfere with her or seek to curb her generosity. Men were not welcomed in their quarters—though he owned the casbah, he only visited the women's quarters by express invitation. "Of course they all live with me. Where else would they live?"

"Do you keep them locked away?"

He thought of the spacious, airy quarters enjoyed by the women of his household, both in his casbah in the country, and the more compact but no less ornate riad he kept for them in town, as well as the beautiful gardens tiled in extravagant mosaics and adorned with fountains set aside for their exclusive use. They had the use of any number of male servants to escort them whenever they wanted to visit the local souk to purchase pretty trifles, or when they wished to visit friends on feast days. "They have every comfort they could wish for. Why do you ask? Do I seem such an ogre to you?"

She shrugged, her face still troubled. "Your ways are different from mine. I was seeking to understand, not to condemn. But still, I do not think I would like it there. I am too fond of my freedom to be happy in a cage, be it ever so prettily gilded."

She needed to walk through the beautiful gardens where his womenfolk lived and bathe in the hammam, the public bathhouse where all the women in the district came to chatter while they steamed and scrubbed. She needed to see the wide-open vistas of his land—the tall mountains and the deserts of golden sand as far as the eye could see. There would be no talk of cages then. "When you come to Morocco, you will see for yourself the ways in which we live."

"When I come to Morocco?" She brushed a stray lock of hair away from her face. "I am sure it is a very pretty place, but I have no plans to visit it on my own, and my employers do not take their children traveling."

"You will find a warm welcome as my guest."

"As your honored guest for as long as I take your fancy?" Her laughter dissolved into the wind. "I am afraid that position does not interest me. It lacks a certain permanence that I would require in such a situation."

Her refusal did not spoil his mood. He would give her so much more than she had ever dreamed of. Once she heard his offer, there would be no more talk of refusing him. "As you have said yourself, your job as a nursemaid is hardly permanent."

"At least it does not spoil me to hold down similar positions in the future. But come, let's not quarrel. You want to be my lover, and despite the impression I may have given you last night, I do not wish it. Let us leave the matter be."

He moved closer to her and put one arm around her shoulder, feeling unaccountably pleased when she did not sidle away from his touch as he had expected. "You are asking me to give up my dream of being with you? That is asking a lot from me."

"On the contrary, *you* are asking a lot from me. You are asking for my innocence."

He traced down the line of her cheek with his forefinger, confident of success. Her skin was as smooth and pale as alabaster. "All I am asking for right now is a kiss. Surely that is not too great a boon for you to grant."

She moistened her mouth with the tip of her tongue, a mute confession that she wanted his kiss. "We are in the garden. Anyone could see us."

He gestured at the empty landscape in front of them. "The children are out with their mother. Everyone else is safely going about their duties in the house. No one would see us." They were quite alone amid the cypress trees—alone enough that he could spread his jacket out on the ground and make love to her without fear of interruption. Not that she would let him go as far as that—not in broad daylight. No, it would take the cover of darkness and secrecy to seduce her from the last of her inhibitions.

"I do not trust you." In her voice he could hear the war between desire and caution. "Will you stop at a kiss? Or will you use it as an excuse for something more?"

"The power is all yours." He took her face in his hands and looked deeply into her eyes. "I will stop whenever you ask me to." He meant every word of the promise he made her. He would not take her if she was unwilling. Only when she wanted it as much as he did, when she was unable to refuse him, would he make love to her.

She leaned back against the cypress tree and let her eyes drift shut. "Then you may kiss me."

A featherlight touch on her mouth, just to taste her. Ah, how sweet she was—sweeter than dates and honey.

His hands caressed her neck and shoulders as he leaned in to taste her more deeply. Her mouth opened under his, her tongue pressing against his.

One touch of her tongue against his was all it took for his shaft to harden. Planting his feet on either side of her, he held her against the tree, his chest touching her breasts, and his erection pushing against the juncture of her thighs. If her gown was just pushed aside, if he were to unbutton his trousers and free his cock, he would be able to slide inside her with one long thrust.

He closed his eyes with the torment of it, being so close to paradise and yet being barred from it. Seducing Louisa was taking all of his self-control. She pushed him to the edge so quickly. Just a simple kiss and all he could think about was fucking her.

He moved his hands to her bodice, deftly unbuttoning it and casting it aside on the grass. Then it was but a moment's work to push her chemise down over her shoulders and free her breasts.

She had beautiful breasts, even whiter and more translucent than the rest of her skin, and tipped with nipples of a rosy pink. Bending his head, he passed his tongue over one of them and watched it pucker into a hard little nub.

"This is what you call stopping at a kiss?" she asked him, breathless, but she did not tell him to stop. Instead, she arched her back, thrusting her breasts forward to beg for more.

He nibbled kisses down the side of her neck, finishing by taking her other nipple into his mouth and sucking on it until it, too, was as tight as it would go. "I am kissing you," he said, standing tall again. "I am kissing you all over."

"Someone will see you." But her protest was weak, and she made no move to cover herself again except to pull him closer.

"Do you want me to stop?" He had to drag the words out. They did not want to come. If he could, he would stay in the garden with Louisa until night fell, and then he would only cease touching her for long enough to take her to his bed in the house, where he could fuck her in comfort.

"Not yet." A wave of pink spread through her face at her admission.

He took her breasts in his hands, rubbing her nipples with his thumbs. "You like it when I do this to you?"

The only answer she gave him was to moan gently, and to rub herself against his cock where it pressed up against her. Her chest was flushed with crimson and her breathing was heavy.

There were other places yet to be kissed. He bent his head to her breasts again, and distracted her with kisses while he pulled her skirts up at the back and slid his hands up to her waist.

Her drawers were tied with a string around her waist. A gentle tug on the string, and they were no longer a barrier to his hands. Her backside was firm and round, and when he leaned right in to run his fingers into the cleft between her legs, he could feel the telltale wetness there.

If he was hot for her, she was equally so for him.

Moving quickly, he shrugged out of his jacket and laid it on the ground in front of her, then sank to his knees, pulled her skirts up to her waist, and started to kiss her thighs.

"What are you doing?"

"Kissing you," he mumbled against her skin, "where you have never been kissed before."

When he reached the patch of curls at the top of her thighs, parted her folds with his fingers, and touched the tip of his tongue to her nub of pleasure, she let out a cry of shocked delight. "I don't think you should be doing this," she said, when she had recovered her breath enough to speak.

What he really ought to be doing was tossing her on the

back of a fast horse and carrying her away with him to Morocco, where he could feast on her to his heart's content. But this would suffice him in the meantime. He thrust her bunched up skirts into her hands. "Hold these for me."

Obediently she clutched her skirts up high enough for him to have unimpeded access to her pussy. The curls that covered her there were fair and delicate, barely thick enough to hide her secrets, and soft and springy under his fingers. He nuzzled his face into them, drinking in the scent of her womanhood, musky and sweet with the wetness of her desire.

With one hand, he gently encouraged her to spread her legs open. Lost in need, she had no will but what he gave her, allowing him to position her with her legs apart and her hips thrust out toward him in invitation.

He explored the cleft between her legs, dipping the tip of his finger into her cunt, and bringing it away again drenched with her juices.

Though he would not take her for the first time in the garden, still he would give her a taste of the pleasure she would receive at his hands, as his mistress. Before he took her back to the house, he would have her trembling in his arms, her desire satisfied. Once she realized what pleasure he could give her, she would be that much closer to fully succumbing to him.

He dipped one finger into her again, moving it in and out of her in a slow, steady rhythm, pushing into her wet pussy and feeling it tighten around his finger. His cock strained against his trousers, longing to replace his finger, but he tamped down his own need with ruthless control. This was about tending to Louisa's needs before his own.

Still fucking her with his finger, he bent his head to her nest of curls. Her nub was hot against his tongue as he licked it, and she shuddered all over as he took it into his mouth.

Her pussy was contracting against his finger so tightly that it was an effort to move in and out of her. She was close to an orgasm; he could feel it in the way she arched into him, in the harsh laboring of her breathing.

He could no longer hold back his own desires. With a speed brought on by desperation, he unbuttoned his trousers and took his cock in his free hand, stroking it with long, hard strokes. This was no time for gentleness.

Louisa gave a cry and her pussy convulsed around his finger, her nub throbbing under his tongue. He held his finger still, deep inside her, as she rode out the waves of her pleasure.

The knowledge that he had given her an orgasm, the first that a man had ever given her, made him lose the remaining vestiges of his own self-control. A few short strokes and he felt his own orgasm approaching. As her pussy throbbed around his finger, he spurted his own come onto the ground between her legs with a groan of utter relief.

Louisa slowly came to herself again. The pleasure that Ithry Khair had given her was so intense that she had been completely lost. He had taken her to the moon and back again, and only now, with her two feet planted firmly on solid ground again, did she realize the enormity of what she had done.

His finger was still deep inside her, and his face was buried in her thatch of curls. Her face burned with embarrassment as she realized the position she was in, her breasts bare, her skirts around her waist and legs spread wide apart. How had she been so carried away that she had allowed him such liberties? It had been a madness in her blood, a few moments of temporary insanity that had robbed her of all her good sense.

Her fingers cramped. With a start of horror she realized that she had held up her own skirts to allow him to touch her so intimately. She dropped them hurriedly, hiding the sight of his head buried in her lap.

He slid his finger out of her, disentangled himself from her skirts, and got to his feet again. She could only look at him with wounded eyes as he tucked his parts away and buttoned his trousers. Lost in her own pleasure, she had not even thought of his.

He turned back to her with an easy smile. "Now then, let us make you tidy again."

With tender care, he slid her chemise back over her shoulders, hiding her breasts, and helped her into her bodice.

His jacket was still lying on the ground. He spread it out and sat down on it, then pulled her into his arms. "Come sit with me for a time, Louisa."

With her clothing repaired, she felt much more at ease. Now, anyone happening upon them by chance would think only that he had perhaps stolen a kiss to put that flush on her cheeks and disarray her hair. They would have no reason to suspect that she had just acted the wanton, and received the most profound pleasure in her life.

Though she was racked by guilt, her body was humming with a satisfaction that made her want to curl up in his arms and sleep. She leaned back against him and let her eyes drift shut. Her lack of sleep began to catch up with her. Surely she would be safe in his company for a few moments. If he had been intent on taking her virginity, he had already had a perfect opportunity this afternoon, while she was so far gone in need that she would have allowed him anything. That he had not done so was once again due to his forbearance, not to her resistance.

She must break herself of this attraction to him, she thought, as she snuggled into his arms. Now that her need for him was satisfied, it would be easier to keep her distance. Her body would no longer betray her as it had today. She would be able to resist him from now on.

A husband and children, in a cottage in the country—that was all she wanted in life, nothing more.

But as modest as her dreams were, fooling around with Khair Bey would put them out of her reach forever. She must not let a moment's pleasure take precedence over her future happiness—even though the pleasure he gave her was enough to intoxicate her very soul.

★ ★ ★

Khair Bey gazed down at the sleeping woman in his arms. A needle from the tree above them had floated down onto her cheek and he blew it off with a soft breath, overcome by a wave of tenderness.

He had given her her first taste of pleasure this afternoon. Though she was still a virgin, he had introduced her to the sensation of a man's touch, of his mouth and fingers working to satisfy her. Soon he would take her to the ultimate pinnacle of pleasure, replacing his finger in her pussy with the thickness and length of his engorged cock, filling her with him, and flooding her with his come.

He would be the first man to breach her, as he had been the first man to give her pleasure.

He squelched the tendrils of guilt he felt at taking her innocence. Despoiling virgins was not his style—before now he had always confined his attentions to those who had no innocence left to lose and no reputation to sully. Louisa had tempted him beyond his ability to resist, but he would not love her and leave her as easily as he had countless others before. No, she was his to keep. She would be his secret treasure.

Lost in pleasant daydreams of Louisa as his established mistress, he barely noticed the time pass by. After no more than half an hour, he nudged her awake.

She sat up straight and blinked her eyes, disoriented from her brief nap.

"Tongues will be wagging if we spend any more time in the cypress grove," he explained, "or I would have let you sleep all afternoon."

With a muttered exclamation, she got to her feet, brushing off her skirts. "Bother. Whatever will Mrs. Botham think?"

He eyed her wrinkled skirts and her mussed hair with a sense of satisfied ownership. "She will think that you have been on a pleasant stroll with a guest," he lied.

Louisa looked at him doubtfully, but she took his arm and together they picked their way down through the lemon trees on the lower slopes of the hill and back to the lawn that led to the house.

As they approached the door, Louisa tugged her arm out of his. "I am a servant here. I do not need your escort."

He took her by the hand, unwilling to let her go just yet, even if it put her reputation in the household at risk. "Maybe not, but I need yours." She would not be remaining here long enough for it to matter. As soon as his business in Italy was completed, he would take her away.

The housekeeper was waiting for them in the entrance. She gave them an odd look at the sight of them hand in hand like lovers, but she did not comment on it. "Khair Bey, Mrs. Winterbottom regrets that she and her husband will not be dining at home with you tonight. They and the children will be staying with a friend they met in town and have sent word for you to join them there, if you are of a mind to. They will not be back until the morning."

He could not have planned it better himself. "Tell the messenger that I have some business matters to attend to, which I will take advantage of their absence to complete. Have an early dinner served to me in my room, if you please."

Mrs. Botham nodded. "Of course, sir. Would you be wanting anything special?"

"Just a plain dinner will be fine, and plenty of it. I find that my walk in the cypress grove this afternoon has awakened my appetite." And he was looking forward with some eagerness to dessert.

"Certainly, sir."

As soon as she was gone, he pulled Louisa around to face him. "So, my dear workingwoman, you have the whole of the evening to yourself, with no children to tend."

She looked down at her shoes. "I will spring clean the nursery while the children are away. I have been meaning to find the time to do it for weeks."

"And leave me to spend the evening alone? That is less than hospitable of you."

"I would be in the way. You have business to do. You said so yourself."

Placing a finger under her chin, he tipped her head back, forcing her to look at him. "Come now, that was merely an excuse to stay behind with you. We shall dine together in my room, and I will show you just a taste of how we live in Morocco."

"We will just dine together?" She leaned closer to him so no listening ears could overhear. "Like this afternoon was just a kiss?"

"And I will kiss you again, if you give me leave," he replied, unperturbed by her whispered accusation. "But I will go no further than you want me to, Louisa. That much I promise you."

Four

In the early evening, when Khair Bey knocked on the door to her room and let himself in without ceremony, Louisa was freshly washed and dressed in her favorite gown, with her hair redone in a style that was less severe than usual. Though she had determined that dining with him in his room was not the most sensible course of action, she knew in her heart that he would never accept her refusal. He would come looking for her and persuade her into it, so she wanted to be ready for him. Her vanity would not let her go to dinner in a soiled gown or with a dirty face, particularly not to an intimate dinner such as he clearly had planned for her.

He looked with approval at her attire. "You look delightful."

She smoothed her hands over her skirts. A present from her brother and sisters, her gown was the pale blue of a robin's egg, with a low-cut bodice and ruffles at the hem. Given that it was not suitable day wear for a nursemaid, she hardly ever had occasion to wear it, but it made such a pleasant change from her usual dull grays and browns. It made her feel as if she were a woman, not just a servant. "Thank you." She was foolishly glad he had noticed it.

"Come, let me take you to my room. I have prepared a surprise for you."

She did not rise from the chair where she sat with her neglected mending on her lap—a last gasp of sanity and self-preservation. "I do not think I should."

"And have all my preparations go to waste?" With one fluid movement, he disposed of her basket of mending onto the floor and pulled her to her feet. "I cannot allow that."

How did he manage to overcome her resistance so easily each time? His will was so strong that her own crumbled before it. "But . . ."

"Not another word," he commanded, as he hustled her along the corridor toward the guest wing. "I shall not be refused."

When he opened the door to his room and ushered her inside, she could not help gasping in wonderment. He had turned the Winterbottom's second-best guest room into an Aladdin's cave of delights. Beautiful red striped rugs were spread out over the floor, and on top of them was a heap of jewel-colored cushions larger than she had ever seen before. On a little low table in front of the cushions stood a group of dishes filled with all sorts of delicacies that she had not tasted in years. Figs, dates, and almonds were all heaped in profusion. The room even smelled different, of exotic spices rather than gas lamps and coal dust. It was as if he had transported her into a different world.

He kicked off his boots and slid his stockinged feet into a pair of red embroidered slippers before sinking down onto the pile of cushions. "Come, join me," he ordered, patting the cushions beside him in invitation. "You must pretend you are in Morocco now, and do as we do in my homeland. It will be good practice for when you come back with me."

She looked askance at him, lounging at ease on the floor. To her English eyes, Moroccan habits did not seem entirely proper. She perched rather hesitantly on the edge of a large cushion, tucking her dress carefully around her ankles before clasping her knees with both arms. "I am not coming to Morocco with you."

"Of course you are. You cannot think I will leave my pretty English rose to wither away in Italy without me?" Khair Bey leaned back, his arms stretched out behind his head, amusement shining in his eyes. "You look like such a prim and proper English miss," he teased, "sitting there as if at any moment you expect me to leap up and bite you. Come, relax a little. You needn't be so stiff and formal as if you were having an audience with the sultana herself. In Morocco we are far less formal. And there are only the two of us here."

That was exactly why she couldn't relax. She'd been mad to give in to his persuasion and come to his room in the first place. What was it about him that made all her common sense desert her the moment he crooked a finger in her direction? It wasn't just his fine words—plenty of other men had tried to charm her into their beds, and none of them had even come close enough to kiss her. It wasn't his promises either—he had made none. There was just something about him that made her want to curl up in his arms and share his warmth.

Even though she knew how dangerous he was to her peace of mind, he made her feel safe. Though she knew how badly he wanted to make love to her, he gave her the power to continue or to withdraw. The choice of how far they went belonged to her and until now he had accepted her withdrawal without argument.

No, it wasn't him that made her nervous—she didn't trust herself. In the heat of the moment, would she make the right choice, the decision that would safeguard her future? Or would she fall headlong into the temptation of pleasure and set her fondest dreams forever out of reach?

"I will just have to make you comfortable in my company. I shall start by feeding you." He reached over, picked up a bowl of figs, and popped one into her mouth.

She savored the sweetness and the texture of the seeds on her tongue as she chewed. Even when her father had been alive, and her family had seen better days, figs were a rare treat. It was almost with regret that she finally swallowed it. "Is this really how you eat in Morocco?"

"Your dinner parties are strange to me. In Morocco, men and women eat their meals apart, unless a man is eating alone with the woman of his heart, and then he feeds her the choicest tidbits from his own hand."

"Eating only in the company of other women would seem strange to me."

He took a handful of almonds and fed them to her one by one. "You will get accustomed to it."

She ate the almonds that he fed to her with as much delight as the fig. If she were able to eat almonds and figs every day, no doubt she could get used to a good many things.

Not, however, to a man who had a harem full of women kept locked away from daylight, she reminded herself. And he had openly proclaimed that he was not married to any of them. Keeping fifty concubines might be a Moroccan custom, but the thought horrified her. Every country had its own way of doing things, but some ways of living were too strange, too immoral, to be able to countenance.

Life in a harem would never be for her, whichever way she looked at it. Not even if Khair Bey were to hand-feed her figs and almonds by the bushel load.

"When you come to Morocco with me, we will travel to the south and there I will feed you fresh dates plucked from the palm trees. There is nothing as sweet on this earth." He leaned over and brushed her cheek with the back of his hand. "Except for you. You are sweeter than dates dipped in honey."

His fulsome praise made her feel uncomfortable. She tightened her arms around her knees, sitting just as a child would. "You are full of foolish words."

"There is nothing foolish about the truth. You are very sweet, and also very beautiful."

"More foolish words. I am too pale to be pretty." Men liked women with pink roses in their cheeks and a healthy glow. She had always been as pale as moonlight. Her seeming availability, not her beauty, is what had kept men sniffing around her.

"Beauty is in the eye of the beholder, and in my eyes you are the loveliest woman I have ever known. I love the pale gold of your hair, and the whiteness of your skin without a single blemish, not even the tiniest freckle to mar its perfection. I love the blue of your eyes, and the way your hips sway when you walk." He brushed his hand over her hair, her face, and down to her hips as he spoke. "Everything about the way you look is what I love in a woman." He paused for a moment, just gazing at her. "So tell me, what do you find beautiful in a man?"

Louisa shrugged, continuing to hug her knees. "I have never thought about it." She would not confess that her mind ran to bronzed skin and dark hair that curled over broad shoulders, and a man too persistent to take no for an answer.

"To me, a beautiful woman has the fresh taste of spring rain, not the musty damp taste of an autumn downpour. Her voice speaks of pleasantness and intelligence, not of meanness or stupidity."

She looked at him, surprised that a man would look for intelligence in a woman. She had always supposed the only thing a man wanted was the treasure between her legs and nothing more.

She knew what he meant when he said that a woman should taste of spring rain. She was sure that some of the men Mr. Winterbottom did business with would have a particularly vile taste, like the dust left after a coal fire has burned itself out. Most of them smelled terribly of stale tobacco and unwashed clothes. And all of them spoke to her as if her head were quite empty, with nothing but air between her ears.

Khair Bey, by contrast, smelled intriguingly spicy—not that she would tell him so. "I suppose a man also needs to taste fresh," she admitted, "but it would have to be a more manly taste than spring rain, a taste that implies strength yet does not taste strong. As for his voice, he would have to speak to me as an equal, not as some sort of dim-witted creature to be ordered around with gruff commands. I have heard men speak more kindly to their hounds than they have spoken to me."

"And have I spoken to you as if you were a dog?"

She could not help grinning at his silly question. "No, I must say you have not. Unless you speak more kindly to your dogs than everyone I know."

"A woman's body should be beautiful as well, to match the beauty of her mind. Her body should not be soft and flabby from a life of overeating and indolence, nor should it be thin and hard from malnutrition or severity of character. In this regard, your body is most beautiful—it is firm where it ought to be firm, yet soft in all the right places."

As he spoke to her in his lilting voice, Louisa felt herself increasingly relaxed in his presence. When she agreed to dine with him, she had feared that as soon as he got her alone in his room, he would immediately start pawing at her clothes; instead, here she sat on a soft silk rug, eating delicious treats and having a pleasant conversation, albeit not one she would normally have with a man.

And she had to admit, for some minutes she had felt the now-familiar dampness between her thighs that was caused by his closeness. She remembered how he had tasted her until her breath came in short pants and every nerve in her body came alive in absolute pleasure. But she ought not to dwell on such things. "I too like a man to have some meat on his bones," she replied hurriedly, to take her mind off her dangerous memories, "but not be fat from an excess of rich living." She could never marry a man with a paunch and fat sausage fingers.

She felt her words rolling on, as if it were not her own voice. It was as though she no longer had control of her own tongue, like when she had been drinking sherry with Mrs. Botham in her sitting room. "And I like a man with strong, fine legs. His . . . his upper muscles should be firm and strong, not soft from too much sitting."

"Upper muscles? Where are they?"

She glared at him. He knew perfectly well what she was referring to and was just teasing her to make her blush.

He rolled over onto his side on the floor, moving closer to her until they were almost touching. "Here, show me these upper muscles to which you refer."

She prodded his left buttock with a hesitant finger. "Here."

"Just there?"

"And here," as she touched his right buttock.

"And how do I measure up?"

Emboldened by the discussion and wanting to tease him in return, she firmly gripped his ass, and then gave him a playful slap. "Quite well, I should say, Khair Bey. Firm and juicy, just as they should be."

He shared a grin with her. "Ahh, I see. Anything else that you like in a man?"

Louisa felt as if she had swallowed down two generous sherries in quick succession, as though the constraints of her entire lifetime were being lifted somehow by the presence of this enigmatic man. Far from being concerned at the thought of dining alone with him in his room, she was starting to feel quite comfortable. He had the knack of putting her at ease.

Moreover, she was feeling a very strong need to touch her pussy—to touch it in the same way that he had with his tongue, softly and in a very sensitive place just above her opening. No, she wanted *him* to touch her there, to stroke her as he had before, to kiss her all over. She had expected that she would have to fight him off, but now that he was making no move on her, she was perversely disappointed. She longed to feel the pleasure he had given her before, to know that he was burning for her as she was for him.

Feeling a slight reddening of her cheeks at her wayward thoughts, Louisa let go of her knees and leaned back on a pile of cushions on the floor, emboldened to say things she had not even dared to think about in all her previous years. "Well, yes, there is more. Personally I am not so enamored of men that are overly hirsute. I would imagine it is not terribly nice to kiss a man's body that is smothered in hair." She shot him a naughty look, daring him to answer her in kind. "How well do you fare in that regard?"

"If I simply told you, would you believe me?"

She looked up and gave him a mischievous smile. "I am too canny to take a man simply at his word. I'm afraid that I would need to determine for myself."

Grinning playfully, Khair Bey unbuttoned his shirt and slowly removed it to reveal a smooth, muscular chest. "Well?"

She knew at that point there was no going back—the last of her defenses crumbled at the sight of the half-naked man lying so close to her, breathing next to her, daring her to touch him. If he still wanted her, she could not refuse him anything.

He was not the pasty, flabby gentleman she thought she would one day marry, but a strongly built man with eyes that shone with the adventure of far-off places. Wrapping her arms around his neck, she kissed him without a word, indicating her submission.

As his soft lips touched hers, she leaned in, trying to get as much of her body as possible into contact with his. Their passionate kiss continued as she ran her hands down his back, around his waist, and then up his chest to his nipples where her fingers played briefly. To her surprise, his nipples became hard little points, much as her own did when he touched them in the same manner.

Before she had tasted half enough of him, he broke their kiss and pushed her back to arms length. "Are you sure this is what you want? You could leave now and I will not lift a finger to stop you. You can spend your evening darning stockings in peace, if that is what you truly want."

She paused, then silently got to her feet, undid the buttons in the front of her dress, slipped it over her shoulders, and let it fall to the floor. Rather than stopping there, she pulled her cotton shift over her head and then started to remove her undergarments. Now that she had made her decision, she didn't want to stop halfway.

Caught by surprise, Khair Bey struggled to keep up, kicking off his slippers and removing his trousers. He lifted one leg quickly to remove his sock, got it caught on his heel, lost his balance, and ended up in an undignified heap on the silk rug with dates scattered around as the heavy brass bowl overturned.

She couldn't help but giggle as he lay sprawled on the floor, wearing nothing but one sock and white silk drawers that came just to his knees.

He burst out laughing, but then stopped as he looked up at her standing over him. She was more beautiful than he had imagined. Then he laughed again when he realized she was dressed nearly identically, wearing nothing but white knee-length pantaloons and one stocking.

He held his hand out, reaching up for her to join him on the floor. Taking the proffered hand, she knelt down beside him, unable to resist running her hands over his chest, and once again gently squeezing his nipples between her thumb and forefinger. His soft moans of pleasure encouraged her to continue.

Taking her hand again, he guided her to the drawstring of his drawers. Her eyes followed her hand, where for the first time she noticed that his drawers were tented by his straining cock. She tentatively touched the topmost part of the tent, and was surprised when it gave a little jump, as if it had a mind of its own. Intrigued, she lightly stroked him over the soft silk; each time she touched him on the very tip, his cock strained more and more against the fabric.

She stopped and looked down at him lying on his back, eyes closed, clearly enjoying the attention.

She, too, was enjoying the attention she was giving him. Wanting to go further, she released the bow of his drawstring and started to slide her hand down his drawers. He lifted his hips slightly to assist, the silky material sliding easily over his smooth skin until the tip of his cock became caught in the waistband. She tugged a bit harder, eager to see him in his naked glory, when suddenly his cock sprang free, bobbing against his flat stomach. Her breath caught in her throat as she stared at his nakedness.

The skin of his cock was a little darker than the rest of him, with the tip forming a prominent head. At the base, looking very delicate nested between his legs, his balls were tight in his

sac. With his drawers around his knees, she temporarily abandoned removing his clothes at the sight of his erection throbbing slightly with the beat of his heart.

With growing confidence, she wrapped her hand around his
hardness. Taking her hand again, Khair Bey guided it up and
down his shaft a few times, showing her how to touch him to
give him pleasure.

Remembering how he had pleasured her with his tongue,
she bent over and tentatively licked at the tip of his cock. He
tasted mildly salty. Intrigued, she bent her head for another
taste of him, licking the full length of his cock.

Judging by his moans of pleasure, he liked it as much as
she had liked him tasting her. With her hand around the base
of his cock, she opened her mouth and engulfed him as far as
she could. He was larger than she had expected, so big that
she couldn't take more than half of him in her mouth. She
wondered how he would feel inside her—if it would hurt the
first time.

"Stand up and let me admire your body. You are surely the
most beautiful woman I have ever seen."

She was not yet ready to let him take control, but she allowed his cock to slide out of her mouth so she could answer.
"Nonsense, you must have seen many women, and many more
beautiful than me."

"It may be that some have greater physical beauty, but with
you it is a combination of many things that add up to perfection.
Where do you suppose my most sensitive pleasure area is?"

He smiled and shook his head as she glanced once more at his cock. "No, not there, but here." He tapped his head. "My brain is where I feel desire. Now stand for me and finish undressing so I can admire you properly."

She stood, blushing slightly at his gaze. Turning away, she lowered her pantaloons to the floor, providing him with a view of her buttocks. She lifted her leg to remove her remaining stocking, certain she could physically feel his eyes looking at her most intimate places.

Turning once more to face him, she was now fully nude. She had always imagined that this moment, the first time she was naked before a man, would be in the safety of the dark and under the bedclothes—not in a well-lit room with silk rugs and cushions on the floor, and a naked man sprawled at his ease in front of her.

Looking down at him, she was surprised to see him touching his cock, stroking with his hand without a hint of embarrassment. His eyes seemed to devour her body as he stared at the soft hair of her pussy.

Her hands seemed to have a will of their own, questing for her sensitive spot as she in turn stared at his hand slowly sliding up and down, reaching occasionally to caress his balls.

With his free hand, he beckoned her to lie down on the soft rug beside him. He leaned over and kissed her deeply before moving down to lightly brush his lips over her nipples. His mouth caused her back to arch in pleasure as he alternately sucked, licked, and then blew a cooling breath across each nipple.

When she thought she could bear no more, he kissed between her breasts, and then made a chain of tickling, nibbling kisses down her stomach, bypassing her pussy to tenderly kiss her inner thighs. She found herself spreading her legs wide as he nibbled his way back up to the opening of her cunt, mutely inviting him to kiss her where she most needed to be kissed.

Lying back, now completely in his power, she allowed him to lift and spread her legs, opening herself to his sight and touch. Her fists clenched into the silk rug in pleasure as he bent his head and licked at her opening, swirling his tongue inside her as far as he could. Just when she thought she had reached the summit of ecstasy, he moved up slightly to suck gently on the hard nub at the top of her cunt. In only a few seconds, her whole body cried out with the overwhelming sensations coursing through her. Her blood pounding in her ears, her nerves singing with the power of her orgasm, she collapsed limply onto the rug, her eyes closed in utter bliss.

Drawing up to his haunches, he looked at her lying before him. She was indeed a delight, inexperienced and yet so in tune with her own body that she was ready to enjoy its pleasures without reservation.

Opening her eyes, she saw him kneeling over her and smiled at the look of need in his eyes. She reached out and touched his cock, which had lost some of its hardness, sliding her forefinger along the underside of its length. She laughed when it gave an involuntary twitch as she touched its sensitive head. Encouraged, she stroked him as she had seen him do to himself earlier, pausing now and then to caress the tight sac between his legs, carefully massaging the two delicate ovals inside.

Within a few short moments he was once again fully hard, his cock angling out from his body, the head faintly purple and bobbing slightly with his pulse.

Knowing the time was right, she guided him between her legs where he rested his cock at the entrance to her wet cunt. He rubbed his cock up and down her opening, her copious juices making the head slick and shiny in the gaslight. Then slowly he slid inside her, stretching her with his thickness. With half his cock buried in her, he pulled out so that once more the shiny purplish head rested just outside her cunt. Once more he slid half in, then out again.

He continued the teasing for several minutes until she could stand it no longer. Reaching out to grab his strong buttocks, she pulled him to her, making him bury his cock completely inside her. There was a moment of hesitation as she was fully penetrated for the first time—a small tearing feeling and then he was in. His cock filled the empty space inside her, giving her a feeling of completeness she had never known before.

He held still for a moment, deep inside her, and then started a slow back and forth rocking, his cock sliding in and out with each thrust. Soon his full length was moving inside her, the head nearly slipping out then plunging full hilt again, filling her with feelings she never knew were in her.

Once more she felt her pleasure intensifying until suddenly she peaked, her hands pulling on his strong back, trying to get him even further inside. She cried out, calling his name, as her body went rigid in ecstasy.

He lay there for a moment, struggling to control his own orgasm. Never had a woman caused him to come so quickly. He was a man who prided himself on his stamina, but on this occasion he could last no longer. Withdrawing from her hot pussy, he rubbed his cock over her sensitive clit until his own orgasm overwhelmed him and his hot seed spurted out, splashing up over her stomach and breasts.

Exhausted, he collapsed on top of her, where he lay for a moment before propping himself up on his elbows. "Thank you, Louisa. You have given me a rare and precious gift. I will treasure it as it deserves to be treasured."

Louisa lay silently next to him as his breathing deepened into sleep. Though her body was sated, her mind was deeply troubled.

So, this was the end of her dreams. She no longer even had the inducement of virginity to entice a respectable man to marry her. There was no point in blaming Khair Bey for seducing her. She would not take the easy way out and accuse him. She had fully participated in her own shame—indeed, she had eagerly welcomed it. In agreeing to meet with him in his room, ostensibly to dine with him, she had knowingly rushed headlong to her own ruin.

The worst thing was that she had wanted him to take her. If he had pulled back or seemed unwilling, she would have fallen to her knees and begged him to come inside her. Her need had been unstoppable. Even now, though he had made her come to an orgasm twice in one night, she could feel the pull of desire for him. The heat of his body lying next to her on the cushions made her pussy wet with wanting him all over again. If he was awake right now, she would pull him close to her and welcome the surge of his cock inside her body, just as she had the first time. Knowing that he was bad for her was no protection against temptation.

The one saving grace was that he had pulled out of her in time, rather than filling her with his seed. No babe would come of this night.

But if she stayed in the Winterbottoms' house and allowed him to seduce her all over again—as she surely would—would he always have the control to pull out of her in time? She had already lost her virginity. Would she one day find herself also with child?

She could not resist him when he was with her—that much was clear. If she was to save herself from falling headlong into a disastrous affair, she would have to leave him. Only when he was far away from her would she be able to think clearly once more.

She edged away from him slowly. He muttered in his sleep and threw out an arm as if to stop her from leaving, but she wriggled away from under it without waking him. From now on, she would keep her distance from him, no matter what it cost her.

She paused before getting to her feet and looked down at his sleeping form. He had been so kind to her, paying her attention, feeding her delicacies, and talking to her as if she were not just a servant. A lock of hair had fallen over his forehead and she brushed it away with a gentle hand. She could almost fancy that she was in love with him.

That foolish thought made her get to her feet with a decided movement. Love was a distraction that a poor nursery maid could ill afford, especially love for a wealthy foreigner who kept a harem full of girls like her in his homeland. If she did not leave him now, she would end up losing everything, including her self-respect.

He looked so alone and vulnerable lying there naked on the cushions. Grabbing a soft wool blanket from the sofa in the corner, she draped it carefully over him so he would not catch cold, and then tiptoed carefully from the room.

Louisa stood in front of Mrs. Winterbottom feeling as if she were a condemned prisoner facing a firing squad. The Winterbottoms had been so good to her and she hated to cause them any grief, but it must be done. Her mind was made up. She had to leave Naples, and the sooner the better.

Mrs. Winterbottom raised her eyebrows at Louisa's silence. "Well, Louisa, what is troubling you? Fidelia told me you wished to speak with me this morning."

"I am handing in my notice, ma'am," Louisa said in a rush of breath. Back in her own bed once more, she had lain awake much of the night thinking about what she should do, and now that she had made up her mind, she was set on her course of action. Leaving the country immediately was the best and surest way to put herself out of Khair Bey's reach. "I am very sorry, I do not mean to cause you any trouble and I will stay as long as you need to find someone else to care for your girls, but I need to return to England as soon as I can."

Something in her face or her voice must have alarmed Mrs. Winterbottom. "Is everything all right? There is no trouble with your family, is there? Are your brother and sisters well?"

"Yes, ma'am, they are all well." She could feel her bottom lip quivering and she willed herself to smile rather than to cry. It was just weariness that was making her so emotional, she told herself—weariness and a deep disappointment in her own weakness, nothing more. "But my sister Beatrice has written yet again of how much she misses me, and I have a desperate desire to return to England. Italy is lovely, but I miss my home badly at this time of year and I have not been back in so long."

Mrs. Winterbottom pursed her lips. "Well," she said slowly, "if that is indeed your decision . . ."

"Oh yes, it is. It has to be."

"I will confess that we have been thinking for a month or two now that we really ought to get the girls a governess, or even to send them away to school, but they seemed quite content with you. I was looking around for a suitable family to pass you on to, and I had thought that with Mrs. Buchanan expecting any day now . . ." She gave a little blush at such plain speaking. "But no matter. If you are determined to return to England, I shall raise no objections."

Louisa gave a tiny smile of gratitude. It had been easier than she had feared to break the news of her departure, and Mrs. Winterbottom did not seem at all put out that she wanted to leave them.

"Mr. Winterbottom will book you a passage, for of course you must go by ship. It is so much more pleasant than the long journey overland, and then you have to get on a boat anyway to get across the channel to Dover. If you want to return to Italy in a month or two, I'm sure Mrs. Buchanan will be pleased to take you on. I shall have a word with her about it. She has often remarked to me how good you are with Hester and Prudence. And then, of course, you could come to visit them with Mrs. Buchanan and her new arrival. How delightful that would be."

Relief that there would be no obstacles put in her way of leaving made Louisa's head spin. "Thank you. You are very kind. I am indeed anxious to be home." Truthfully speaking, she was only anxious to leave Naples, but it amounted to the same thing.

Mrs. Winterbottom took her hand and gave it a maternal pat. "If you are that desirous of leaving right away, we can find you a merchant ship to sail on in short order. I shall have Mr. Winterbottom look into it right away."

Louisa left the room feeling as if a weight had been taken off her shoulders. She would be able to remove herself from temptation and return to England, to safety, and nurse her wounds in peace.

Khair Bey was a threat to her—a bigger threat than he would ever acknowledge. She was nothing to him; she *could* be nothing to him but a pleasant pastime. He was wealthy and powerful; she was poor and dependent on her position as a nursery maid to live. Even now, if she were to find herself pregnant, he would go on his merry way, while she would have to suffer the consequences of her foolishness for the rest of her life.

She shut her eyes and breathed deeply to dispel the panic that threatened to overcome her at the prospect. There was no sense in dwelling on the risk she had run. She had only succumbed to his seduction once, and she was sure he had pulled out of her in time. Fate would surely not be so unkind as to punish her that harshly for just one mistake, a mistake that she was trying so hard to remedy.

As for his offer to take her back to Morocco with him, she felt her gorge rise at the thought. To be immured in a harem with fifty other women, all of whom he had taken to his bed? It seemed to her to be a vision of a living hell. How she would hate the other women for taking even one fraction of his attention away from her. How jealous she would be when he called on one of them instead of her to share his evening meal and then his bed. She could not even begin to guess how they managed to share one man among so many. She could not live like that. Not even for him. *Especially* not for him.

Her eyes teared over. She could not adapt to his world. His

ways were too foreign to her. Neither could she imagine him striding down the streets of London in his embroidered waistcoat and his red fez. Even in sunburned Italy he looked exotic, but on the drab, gray streets of London he would stand out like a purple and blue peacock among a bunch of gray geese. And just imagine the horror of his neighbors if he were to bring his harem with him!

No, it was best this way. She would cut herself off from him with a short, sharp shock, and then she could get on with the business of healing. It would hurt less in the long run than the gradual fading of her hopes and the eventual destruction of her heart, which would be pulled to pieces one strand at a time.

Given enough time, she would forget about him. She would unlearn the texture of his skin, the taste of his body, and the touch of his hands. No longer would she pine for the sight of him striding toward her, his proud head held high, or for the warmth of his body cradling her in the night.

She had to keep telling herself that, or she would go mad.

Khair Bey slept late that morning, his entire body sated by the lovemaking he had finally enjoyed with his pretty Louisa. She was everything he had known she would be, and more. While the sex had been more explosive than he had ever experienced before, he had not expected to feel such a pull of tenderness toward her, a desire to protect her from the world, to cherish her. He was not the type of man to feel anything for his casual amours other than a passing fancy and a need for satisfaction.

He had been right in thinking that one night with her would never be enough for him. She had crept under his skin and become so much more than a casual romp, even more than a mistress. He needed her as he had never needed a woman before.

His mother was always hinting at his duty to marry. Maybe he should just marry Louisa and be done with it. Her sweet temper meant that she would be easy to live with, and she would be a good mother to their children. True, she came of humble stock, but what did that matter to him? He had no need of more wealth, and no interest in marrying the pampered daughter of a powerful bey who would expect him to dance attendance on her at every turn.

Why hide her away in Medina as his mistress and risk losing her to another man, when he could wed her and live with her as publicly as he pleased. The more he thought about it, the better he liked the idea.

The elders of his village would be displeased if he took her back to Morocco as his wife. They did not approve of the young men hankering after foreign women, but once they had met Louisa and seen her sweetness for themselves, they would understand his fascination with her.

Whatever their reaction would be, he had made his decision. She belonged to him now, and he would keep her.

He rolled over to take her in his arms and was greatly disturbed to find the cushions by his side empty. He had expected to wake up next to her, to see her hair tousled by sleep as she lay beside him, and to feel her body languid with the remnants of the night. Her languor would not have lasted for long in the face of his eagerness to touch her and taste her once more.

But she wasn't there. Suddenly he was utterly awake, raising himself up on his cushions to see if she had merely gotten up for some fresh air.

The silence in the room told its own story. She was gone. He flung the blanket off with a mumbled curse. Was she so ashamed of being his lover that she had to creep away like a thief in the night from his room? Surely she was not the only servant in the house to occasionally wake up in a bed-chamber that was not her own. It was too late for modesty now—she had given herself to him completely, and he had loved every inch of her. To pretend otherwise was nothing more than a lie.

He glanced down at himself, his usual early morning erection prouder and thicker than was common. His body was more than ready to love every inch of her all over again—with every inch of him.

Though he wanted nothing more than to chase her down, right here and now, he reluctantly admitted that he was a guest in another man's house and proprieties ought to be observed. Unfortunately for his peace of mind, he could not go rampaging through the corridors demanding Louisa's whereabouts. Such antics would hardly help him to find favor in her eyes, or in the eyes of his rather reluctant host.

With gritted teeth, he washed and attired himself for the day with as much care and punctiliousness as usual, before descending to take his breakfast coffee with Mr. Winterbottom as though nothing unusual had happened.

Louisa's time would come, he vowed silently, as he downed a hearty breakfast of scrambled eggs and smoked kipper in the company of his host. He would make sure that she realized her place was with him—all the night through.

Though the morning was warm and sunny, she was not in the garden playing with the children as he had expected. A streak of disappointment shot through him. He loved to watch her with the children; she treated them with such love and kindness, they could not help but blossom under her care. They responded to her warmth with artless affection, treating her as they would a treasured big sister.

A picture flashed through his mind of Louisa playing with her own children—with their children—two golden-skinned imps with his dark hair but her clear blue eyes. As much as she loved the two little girls in her care, she would love her own even more. They would be hers, as Prudence and Hester never could be.

The image tugged at his heartstrings. He wanted children to carry on his name, to keep a piece of himself alive long after he was gone. Louisa would be his wife, the mother of his children. No other woman would do.

Of course, he had to find her first, and inform her of his decision. So far, she was proving to be annoyingly elusive.

She was not in the garden, nor was she sitting with Mrs.

Winterbottom in the parlor. When he peeked in the door of the nursery, the room was empty. The housekeeper had not seen her, and neither had the cook. They looked at him suspiciously when he inquired about her whereabouts, but he did not elaborate on his reasons for seeking her. The whole household would know soon enough that he had laid claim to her. Until then, as a bey, he was above explaining his actions.

Irritated by his failure to find her, he let himself into her room and sat down to wait. She could not avoid him for long. Sooner or later she would find him there, and he would make his position clear.

He did not have long to wait. Before the bell had rung for the midday meal, Louisa came into her room. She started at seeing him there. "Do you make a habit of intruding where you are not wanted?" she asked snippily. "Go on, shoo. I have work to do."

Her eyes were red, as if she had been crying. He wanted to take her into his arms and kiss her, tell her that everything would be alright and that he would protect her, but with the mood she was in, she would only rebuff him. "Do you make a habit of running away from your lover in the middle of the night, leaving him to scour the house for you the next morning?" he asked instead.

"You are not my lover; you are merely . . . merely . . ." Lost for words, her voice tailed off into silence.

"Merely the man who took your virginity?" he suggested. "The man in whose arms you spent last night, screaming with pleasure? The man who gave you a taste of heaven in his arms?"

She made an impatient movement with her hands, as if she wanted to brush away the memory. "Merely a foolish fling, a passing fancy, an aberration—nothing more."

"Do you take all your passing fancies to bed with you?" He shook his head in mock reproof. "I cannot think your employers would be pleased to hear of such conduct taking place in their household. Their sweet, innocent nursemaid, the guardian of their innocent daughters, proving herself no better than a whore." His words were hard and cruel, but he found her dismissal of their lovemaking harder and crueler than anything he could say.

"It would not matter. I have handed in my notice this morning. I no longer have a position here."

A smile of triumph lit his face. So, despite her protests to the contrary the previous evening, and despite her argument just now that he had merely been a passing fancy, she had decided to come to Morocco with him after all. He was glad to see her already so reconciled to her destiny. He'd not expected his victory to be so easy, but her capitulation was no less sweet for all its speed. "You will not be sorry. Morocco is a beautiful country and I will take good care of you there."

"You misunderstand me. I am going back to England."

He looked at her, not comprehending at first what she was telling him. She could not be saying that she was leaving him. Then realization dawned. "You want to visit your homeland before you come to mine?" It was a natural enough desire, he supposed, though her timing could be better. After dallying in Italy longer than expected, he needed to get back to Morocco with the profits of his rug selling for his people as soon as he could. Besides, Italy was all very well, but he was missing his own country and his own people. There was no place like home when the intense heat of the summer days started to fade into the cooler evenings of autumn.

"I am not going to Morocco with you. Not now, and not later. I am going back to England." It was a simple statement, uttered with no fuss or fanfare.

Did she really think she could brush him off that easily? He was a descendant of pirates, and only too used to getting his own way. A simple slip of an English girl would hardly present a challenge to him. "I will not allow it."

Her refusal was nothing but her foolishness talking, the understandable nervousness of a young woman about to embark on a new life in a foreign country with a man who was still a stranger to her in so many ways. Didn't she know that he would protect her and see to her safety, wherever she went? It was his duty—and it also would be his pleasure—to keep her happy.

She smiled at him then, a sad smile that tugged at his heart. He stepped forward to take her into his arms, to whisper words of love into her ear, to make her see that she belonged with him, and to put a real smile back on her face. There was no need for sadness now that they were together.

She almost stumbled in her haste to move backward out of his reach. "You have no say in the matter. The decision is mine to make."

"You are promised to me. That gives me every right to have a say."

"We shared a night together. I made no promises to you, nor did you to me."

Was she being deliberately obtuse? "I asked you to return to my homeland with me. Is that not promise enough for you?"

"You forget that I did not accept."

"Marry me, Louisa." He put all his powers of persuasion into the question. "Come to Morocco as my wife."

"I will not marry you." To his dismay, she seemed to shudder at the very thought of it.

"Did last night mean nothing to you, then?" He did not believe her, *could* not believe her. She had given the gift of her chastity to him, the most precious thing she could ever have bestowed on him. How could she have remained unmoved, or treat it now as if it were of no matter? It was simply not possible.

Her threat to leave him now was irrational, completely senseless. He could not understand why she would even think such thoughts, let alone utter them out loud.

"It was a mistake, nothing more."

"A mistake?" Louisa was calling their glorious night together a mistake? In all seriousness, she was calling her gift to him nothing more than a mistake, when he would cherish it for the rest of his life. Her words both insulted and offended him. If she were a man and a member of his tribe, he would have her punished for less.

"And one that I do not intend to repeat."

He held out his hand to her, hating the way she shrank from his touch as if he were poison. "Louisa," he said, and then stopped, not knowing what else to say to her. He did not understand her mood this morning. Was she so proud that she wanted to make him beg for her favor?

He was a bey, the leader of his people. Beys did not beg. They commanded, and people obeyed them without question. "Come here to me."

At his tone of command, she shuffled a fraction closer to him, but not close enough for his liking. "Closer."

She shook her head mutely and remained where she was.

He spoke gently but firmly to her, as if he were speaking to a small child. "I will conclude my business here in Naples as soon as I can and we will leave for Morocco within the week. I will not leave you here. I will take you back with me. There will be no more of this nonsense that you are going to England."

There, that should settle the matter. He had made his wishes plain.

Five

Five short days later, Louisa lay on her hard bunk in a tiny cabin on a merchant ship bound for Bristol. It was done. She had left Khair Bey, for all his blustering, and she was on her way home. In just a little while, she would be back in England and would see all her family again. She was especially looking forward to seeing Beatrice, the sister closest to her in age, and the one she missed the most. It had been too long since she had seen her, too long since she had seen all her family.

The prospect of a reunion with her beloved brother and sisters ought to make her feel happy, but truthfully, she was utterly miserable. For the first time in her life she had fallen in love, passionately and hopelessly in love, and with the most unsuitable man she could ever hope to find. No kindly steward or handsome young footman for her, who would marry her and settle down in a cottage in the country where they would raise a family together. Instead, she had to fall in love with a wealthy foreigner whose idea of a "happily ever after" ending was to cart her off to join all his other women in a harem, where she would become little more than his slave. Truly, she was a fool.

The ship rose up another swell then dropped down the other side and she felt her stomach heave. Traveling by ship was nasty. How she wished the Winterbottoms had booked her passage in one of the new steamships, rather than this old sailing ship. Her trip then would have been half as long, though it would have cost her more. They had already been wallowing in heavy seas for a day and a night on end, and there was no relief in sight.

She could not even go outside to feel the salt spray on her face and get out of the noisome air in her berth for fear that she would slip on the wet decking and fall overboard. After feeling sick for so long, it was doubtful whether her legs still had the strength to hold her upright.

She really ought to have refused Mrs. Winterbottom's offer of a berth on one of her husband's ships, and made her way slowly overland to Calais. It would have taken three times as long, but not half as hard on her poor stomach, and now that she was safely away from Khair Bey, she was in no particular hurry to reach England.

It was the motion of the ship rising and dipping on the waves that made her feel so dreadful—there was nothing more to it. Nobody could feel cheerful when they were so seasick they could not eat or drink without retching. Her misery over Khair Bey would disappear as soon as she was on dry land again. The way she was feeling now, she would welcome falling into the sea if it would mean some relief from her queasy stomach.

Her misery was interrupted by a knock on the door. The captain poked his head around the corner. "Excuse me, Miss, we're just going to heave to and lower the sails, so don't be alarmed if the ship starts wallowing with a bit of a beam sea running. We've sighted a ship that's flying distress flags and we're obliged to offer assistance."

She didn't understand much of what the captain had said except the part about wallowing, which didn't sound very pleasant. It wasn't. Soon the familiar rise and fall of the ship under way was replaced by an even worse side-to-side motion that seemed to swirl her stomach around in every way imaginable.

She was so miserable that she didn't even hear the noise of shouting and cursing up on the deck at first. Not until the sound of a pistol shot reverberated through her cabin walls did she notice that anything was amiss. She sat up weakly on her bed, but the movement made her head swim and her stomach heave. Hoping to keep her sickness at bay, she reached for the glass of water sitting in its little holder on the tiny table to rinse out her mouth.

The noise of shouting and cursing was louder now—she wondered how she had missed it before. Maybe the sailors had mutinied. Or maybe they had hit a reef and were sinking and the pistol shot had been a warning to everyone to take to the lifeboats.

Sick as she was, she didn't want to drown in this miserable stretch of water if she could help it. Moving carefully, she swung her legs over the edge of the bunk and lowered herself to the ground. The ship bucked under her and she grabbed on to her bunk for balance.

It wasn't so hard to move about once she got the hang of it. As long as she kept hold of something with at least one hand to steady herself when the floor suddenly dipped from under her, she could manage reasonably well.

She pushed open the door to her cabin and looked out into the hold, stuffed high with bales of material bound for England. Threading her way through the merchandise, she came to the hatchway that led to the upper deck.

Just as she reached it, it opened and the captain, his face gray with fear, came tumbling down to fall at her feet.

His clear distress made the butterflies in her stomach multiply a thousandfold. She grabbed at the sleeve of his jacket as he passed. "What's wrong?" The lump of fear in her throat almost prevented her from speaking. "Are we sinking?"

He ignored her question, shook off her arm, and darted into his own cabin, coming out again with a pistol in his hand. "Get back into your cabin and lock the door," he said brusquely as he passed. "If they catch sight of you, you would be better off dead."

Captive

She stared after him as he climbed back up through the hatchway, brandishing his pistol as he went. "What's wrong? If who catches sight of me?"

"Barbary pirates. They've boarded us." With that, he kicked the hatchway shut behind him.

Louisa stared after him, rendered motionless with horror. Pirates? Mr. Winterbottom had assured her that the danger from pirates was long gone, and he had never lost a ship or even a part of his cargo to the renegades who had once patrolled the Straits of Gibraltar preying on any hapless ship who needed to pass through the narrow stretch of water that separated Spain from the northern tip of Africa.

The waters of the Mediterranean, he had claimed, were now as safe as his own back garden. Sailing to England on a merchant ship would be as pleasant and relaxing as taking a cruise and the sea air would be beneficial to her weak lungs. By the time she reached England, she would be positively bursting with health.

Now her ship was being boarded by Barbary pirates? She felt sick to her stomach all over again, and this time it had little to do with the lurching of the boat.

So much for Mr. Winterbottom's assurances. The journey seemed less like a pleasant cruise and more like a waking nightmare with every passing minute, and her lungs were bursting with fear, not with health.

She turned on her heel and made her way back to her cabin as quickly as she could, bolting the door behind her with trembling hands. The captain was right—she would be better off dead than as the captive of those barbarians. Heaven only knows what they would do to her if they found her on board. She would surely be raped, and then have her throat slit and be flung over the side to feed the fishes—if they didn't torture her first for their own amusement.

She sat on her bunk, her knuckles white with tension. She willed herself not to let the least sound of fear escape her. Her only hope lay in being as quiet and still as a mouse and escaping their notice.

As she sat there in terror, the noise and the shouting gradually died down overhead. The only sounds she could hear were the slapping of the water against the wooden hull of the ship, the thud of the sailors' feet on the deck above her, and the creak of the ropes and the groan of the sails in the wind.

The captain had not fired his pistol, but she didn't know if that was a good sign or a bad one. Maybe the crew had been overpowered at once and the pirates were in charge of the vessel. Or maybe the captain and crew had frightened them off by putting up a good resistance, and they had left to seek easier prey. While she was still in doubt, she did not dare to unbolt her door to see what was happening. Even if the fighting was not yet over and the crew needed her help, she had no weapon and would only be in the way. The cabin was her only protection.

Just as she was starting to think that the danger might all be over, there was a heavy knock on her door. She froze, petrified, until she heard the voice of the captain. "Are you all right in there, Miss?"

"Yes." Her voice was little more than a squeak. She cleared her throat and tried again. "Yes. I'm fine." The relief of knowing that the captain was alive and well almost made her faint, and she hurriedly put her head between her knees to stop the blackness from overtaking her. The crew must have repelled the pirates and scared them off without a shot being fired.

Her door handle rattled, but the bolts held it shut. "Unbolt your door."

A couple of deep breaths and she almost felt normal again. She got to her feet, hanging on to the bunk for balance. At least her fear seemed to have chased away her nausea for the moment. She could be thankful for small mercies. "Are the pirates gone now? Is everyone safe?"

"Everything is fine now, Miss." The captain's voice sounded oddly strained. She supposed it was the aftereffect of having pirates board his ship and try to make off with his cargo.

She unbolted her cabin door and swung it open.

Outside stood a group of dark-skinned men in loose shirts belted at the waist over baggy trousers—not the ship's crew. One of them held the captain tightly with his arms pinioned behind his back, and with a jagged-looking knife at his throat.

Louisa gasped with fear and tried to slam the cabin door

shut again, but she was not fast enough. One of the men put his booted foot in the way so the door would not close. His foot in the door, he grinned at her, his teeth a wicked slash of white in his face.

Though she leaned all her weight against the door, she could not hold them back. Several of them pushed the door open and crowded inside the cabin, their eyes firmly fixed on her, as if she were a great treasure.

She backed into a corner, her arms crossed in front of her as if she could ward off the intruders with the strength of her will. Her worst nightmare had become her new reality. The captain had betrayed her.

All her feeble efforts to protect herself were of no use. Before she could do anything more than whimper in fright, her arms were tied behind her with a piece of dirty rag, and she was being manhandled out of the cabin.

"I'm sorry, Miss," the captain cried, as she struggled vainly against her captors. "They were too strong for us. As soon as they heard there was a woman passenger on board, they threatened to murder my crew and then set fire to the ship if I did not do as they asked. There was no hope for you either way, but by giving you up at least I get to save my men."

She knew that he had lied to her to save his own life. The smell of fear clung to him like a second skin. "What will they do with me?" she asked, twisting around to read the truth in his face.

He could not meet her eyes. "I'm sure they will treat you

well. Pretty young women are highly prized all along the Barbary Coast. They will not want any harm to come to you or they will lose their profit."

The meaning of his words sunk into her with enough force to take all the air out of her lungs. She'd wondered why the hold, as they passed through it, had seemed as crowded as before, when she had expected it to be despoiled and empty of anything of value. Now she knew. The pirates had not bothered with the cargo of fabric because they already had the most valuable item on board—at least in their eyes. They were going to sell her as a white slave—for what nefarious purpose she could guess only too easily.

She threw an anguished glance at the captain as the pirates shoved her through the hatchway and out onto the deck. He was allowing her to be taken, knowing the dreadful fate that awaited her. She wanted to scream at him in rage and disgust. What kind of a weasel let a woman under his protection be taken off into servitude by pirates? Had he been a real man, he would have fought for her liberty instead of giving in without striking a single blow in her defense.

It was the first time she had been out on the deck since they had sailed out of the harbor. The sea rose and fell in big, rolling swells, taking the ship—and her balance—with it. Despite her days on the ship, she could not gain her balance on the slippery wooden deck. Though she stumbled and grabbed at whatever she could for support, her captors hurried her onward to the railing.

Standing on the edge and clinging to the rail, she could see nothing but ocean as far as the horizon—no land, nothing but a vast blue emptiness. That is, except for the pirate ship, afloat some distance away.

She blinked in disbelief as she looked at it. For a pirate ship, it appeared remarkably similar to the merchant ship she had been traveling in. It was the same general size, though its masts were taller and it looked lighter and faster. The ship gave out an air of menace, as though it was built for stealth and speed. It wasn't flying the skull and cross-bones, an obvious sign of its nefarious intentions, but a deep red flag the color of blood.

There were no other sails in the distance to offer the hope of rescue—no one to call for help; nothing but despair. The pirates motioned for her to climb over the rail, and looking down into the heaving sea, she saw a small boat with four rowers, their oars vertical in the air, as a fifth man clung to a rope ladder, holding the rowboat steady against the side of the ship.

With a sword at her back, Louisa eased over the railing, her knees weak with fright and her knuckles white from the effort of hanging on. The sea yawned hungrily below her. She shut her eyes tightly, both hoping and fearing that she would fall and find a swift death in the embrace of the cold waves. It would be a kinder fate than spending the rest of her life as a slave of some barbaric Barbary prince.

Somehow she managed to descend the ladder, and then fell

the last short distance into the longboat, where one of the men caught her. The remaining pirates scuttled down the ladder with ease and pushed off from the sailing ship. As they rowed toward the pirate ship she looked back at the merchant ship in complete terror, certain her life would soon come to an end.

Her emotions drained and her body numb with despair, she lay in the bottom of the little boat as it came alongside the pirate ship. Unable to move, she was carried over the shoulder of a pirate like a sack of wheat and lifted up onto the deck. As she was carried across the deck, she looked up and thought she saw a familiar face.

Surely that was not Khair Bey standing at the helm? She shook her head to clear her vision. When she looked again, the figure was gone—if it had ever been there in the first place. Her imagination must be playing tricks on her and showing her what she wanted to see. They were close to the coast of North Africa where he came from, and there must be many men who resembled him here.

The vision of his face gave her new courage to fight against her captors, but all her efforts were in vain. Though she struggled to be released, she was carried down into the hold of the pirate ship with no ceremony and dumped not too harshly on the bunk bed of another tiny cabin.

With a smile that she wasn't sure was meant to reassure or terrify her, her captor backed away and left her alone, bolting the door behind him from the outside.

She quickly took stock of her surroundings: a wooden bunk nailed to the floor so it would not move during a storm; a mattress made of ticking, covered in a couple of rough blankets; and an empty sea chest, also nailed to the floor. There was nothing at all that she could turn into a makeshift weapon.

She tested the door. It was firmly bolted, as she had suspected. There was no way out of her cabin until her captors chose to release her. In any case, the longer her door stayed firmly bolted during the voyage, the safer she would be.

Sitting on the bunk, she took several deep breaths to calm the pounding of her heart. Her relief at finding herself safe for now, instead of being raped by a dozen fearsome pirates, was tempered by her terror of what the next few days would bring.

She had heard stories of what Barbary pirates did to the women they captured. The prospect made her shudder with fear and disgust.

Her best chance was to act like a virgin, even to outright lie if she must. Untouched women fetched a far higher price on the slave market, so everyone said, and the pirates, however savage they might be, would surely want to gain the highest profit from her capture. If they were to find out she was less valuable than they had hoped, she would surely suffer the worst kind of mistreatment at their hands before they disposed of her.

★ ★ ★

Khair Bey strode across the deck of his fastest trading vessel. "Well?" he demanded of the rough-looking men who came up from the hold. "Have you secured her? Is she safe?"

Unable to be part of the boarding party, he had watched the whole process from the ship's wheel. He had seen the sailors capitulate without a fight, and then watched as Louisa was taken up on deck, shivering with terror and stumbling in the rolling sea.

The look of fear on her face as she was brought aboard his ship made his insides knot, but did not weaken his resolve. Come what may, he had to have her. Her intransigence had forced him to make this move.

His second mate grinned in triumph. "It went just as you said it would. The merchants were only too eager to give her up in exchange for their ship and the rest of their cargo—and with only a single warning shot fired. She's safely aboard."

The cowardice of the merchant sailors, who would give up a woman to reputed Barbary slavers in exchange for their ship, made him grind his teeth with fury. It was tempting to fire a cannonball or two into the side of their vessel to teach them a lesson. Still, he had counted on that very cowardice to deliver Louisa to him, and in that he had not been disappointed. "Unharmed, I trust? I warned you I will have the hide of any man who treats her roughly."

"The men were as gentle as lambs with her."

"Good. Now go and keep a watch outside her cabin. Take her food and water, but otherwise she is to remain undisturbed until we get into port. I will not have her frightened any more than is necessary. And get some men over the side to return the ship to her original name."

The man hurried off to do his bidding, and Khair Bey resumed his striding up and down the deck. Her refusal to take his suit seriously had forced him to take drastic measures.

His ancestors had been pirates. Returning briefly to the trade that had made his family wealthy seemed like the obvious plan.

By intercepting the ship in which she'd been traveling, he'd run the risk of being apprehended and hung as a pirate, but that part of his plan had been executed flawlessly. All that remained was for him to come riding to her rescue, and to reap the reward of her gratitude that would surely follow. In time, her gratitude would deepen into love, and then she would belong to him forever.

She already liked him as a man—no innocent could have feigned her reaction to him. But that had not been enough to keep her by his side. He needed more than her desire—he needed her affection, too. There was so much love in her to give, and he wanted her to give it all to him. He was jealous of even the tiniest crumb of her attention, of the smallest reason she might have to leave him again.

She would come to no harm under his protection. He had given strict instructions she was not to be touched.

Once she had a reason to be grateful to him, she would no longer be able to resist him. She would be his, utterly and completely. He would have conquered her.

The thought made him stand taller and prouder than ever. Though she might not know it yet, he had captured his woman. He would make up for his deception a thousand times over. She would belong to him in body and soul, and he would take care of her and protect her until the end.

Louisa sat alone in her cabin for hours, her fear and isolation broken only by one of the pirates bringing her food and water, and emptying her chamber pot. Her face burned at the need to have her personal needs taken care of by such a rough man, but there was no help for it. He did not offer her any further insult, and for that she was grateful.

Though her appetite was completely gone, she forced herself to swallow the food and water that was brought to her. She would need her strength in the days to come. The food at least was good, though spicier than she was used to and with interesting new flavors; even the water was remarkably fresh, untainted by any brackish taste.

Most of the time, she sat on the bunk in the hot, humid, salt-infused atmosphere of her cabin, wishing for a window to open to catch a breath of fresh air. Thankfully, her seasickness had not returned, so she was spared that misery at least.

The waiting was the worst part. There was nothing to do but deal with the demons in her mind. Despite her relative safety on board the ship, she found herself longing for the hour when they disembarked. Whatever horrors awaited her on land, it would mark an end to the waiting.

She was asleep, lying back on the bunk and dreaming of the cool, clean shores of England, when they came for her. Her cabin door opened, letting in a draft of stale air from the hold and she sat up, groggy and disoriented from sleep.

The pirate grabbed her by the elbow and growled a few words in a language she did not understand. His meaning, however, was clear. She was to get up and go with him.

Pushing him away, she clambered to her feet and brushed her skirts down. Her legs were shaking, but she forced them to hold her upright. Whatever her fate was, she would face it on her feet, and with her head held high. The pirates may have captured and enslaved her, but they would not touch her soul—that belonged to her alone. She would not let these barbarians see her fear.

It was dusk when her captor brought her up to the deck. They had docked in a small fishing port, surrounded on all sides by brightly painted fishing boats with nets hanging over the sides to dry. The stragglers were still unloading their catch of the day onto the wooden wharf that stretched out along the water's edge. Others wore turbans of blue and red and sat cross-legged on the decks in the fading light, mending holes in their nets. The smell of fish hung everywhere in the air.

Louisa looked around, her hope of escape fading fast. Even if she were to run, there was nowhere to go. The fishermen looked almost identical to the pirates who had captured her. Probably they were all pirates when it suited them, supplementing their income from fishing with a rare, more lucrative, catch.

She would have tried to escape anyway, throwing herself on the mercy of any local woman who looked as if she might take pity on a stranger. Surely, no woman could stand by and watch one of her own sex enslaved and about to be handed over to a dreadful fate without at least trying to help. To her distress, however, she did not see a single woman on the wharf, let alone one who might have the power or influence to save her.

No wonder her captors had not even tied her hands together. Why waste good rope when she was trapped?

The pirate at her elbow jostled her over the deck and onto the wharf.

Only then she did she look up and see the town, gleaming white against the hillside. Despite her fear, her heart caught in her throat. The square white buildings clustered on the slopes and spread out over the flatland to the edge of the sea, all of them dwarfed by a red brick tower that rose high above the sea of white. The sight took her breath away with its exotic beauty and its strangeness. For all its nearness to Spain, the Barbary Coast had a very different feel to it than the Europe to which she was accustomed.

She hardly had time to take in more than a glimpse of the town before her captors surrounded her on all sides and hurried her along the wharf. Other than the one who had her by the elbow, they were all carrying large bundles on their shoulders.

Booty from their piracy, she thought sourly. Fine jewels and clothing that rightfully belonged to other men, no doubt. She hoped they would get no joy from their pillaging.

She could see little more than the backs of the men in front of her as they strode along. After several days of sickness and fear on the sea, her legs felt like India rubber and she had to scramble to keep up with the pace.

The wooden wharf gave way to a dirt-packed roadway where a cluster of donkeys stood patiently to one side. Her captors made straight for the animals and began to load their bundles onto the beasts of burden. She knew exactly what they thought of her when she too was unceremoniously picked up and dumped on the back of one of the poor donkeys, just as if she were another piece of booty.

She grabbed at the thick rug covering the donkey's back to keep her balance as her captor pulled on the rope tied to the donkey's halter, and the beast unhurriedly moved off with its fellows.

In a slow procession, they moved through the town, winding along streets so narrow she could almost reach out and touch both sides at once. The air was heavy with moisture, and no cooling breeze found its way through the maze of winding paths that made up the town.

On both sides of the roadway were huge walls of plaster towering high above her, painted blue or green around the bottom and white at the top, interspersed with the occasional heavy studded door. The walls seemed to close in on her until she could barely breathe.

Captive

The donkeys shuffled to a stop outside one of the doors, and one of the pirates banged forcefully with the iron knocker.

Slowly, the door opened inward, leaving just enough space for the donkeys to amble through a dark vestibule into a large, tiled courtyard. A fountain stood in the middle, the lilting music of its water making her realize how thirsty she was. She licked her lips as she stared at it, wondering if the water was fit to drink.

Though it was rapidly getting dark, the air was still warm and she felt almost stifled in her corset, gown, and leather boots. Heat, exhaustion, and thirst were seeping into her bones as if they would never leave.

Her captor reached up to lift her down off the donkey, but she pushed him aside and slid down on her own. Despite the black spots of exhaustion that danced in her eyes, her pride would not allow her to accept a common courtesy from her abductors. Her dismount was hardly dignified, but she did not fall.

The gate clanged shut behind them with a heavy thud. So, this courtyard was to be her new prison? At least it did not stink of salt and fish, and move under her feet with every swell, as the ship had done.

An elderly woman bustled toward her, the first woman she had seen since they arrived. Her long robe was tied in the middle with a tassel, and the colorful scarf that covered her head looked strangely out of place on her face, which, though discolored and spotted with age, had originally been as white as Louisa's own. The older woman stared unashamedly at Louisa. "So, you are the prize that came in on the last ship?" Her words, though strangely accented, were in perfectly understandable English.

Louisa gasped in surprise. "You are an Englishwoman?" It was the last thing she would have expected to find in this strange, out-of-the-way place.

"Never you mind," the woman replied sharply, gesturing at Louisa to follow her into the house. "I belong here now, so don't you be trying any of your weepy tricks on me. I've come across all sorts of young women in my time, and I don't have any truck with that sort of behavior." She stopped in the doorway to catch her breath and fixed Louisa with a gimlet eye. "And don't even think about asking me to help you. You're nothing but a piece of merchandise to me, and you'll be helping me to turn a pretty profit."

Louisa stumbled after her, the shock of finding herself with another Englishwoman in this strange place almost robbing her of the power of speech. "What are you going to do with me?"

"The same as I'd do with any woman in your situation. Give you a bath." She gave a wheezy laugh at her own wit. "None of the wealthy gentlemen that my house caters to would take a second look at you despite your pretty coloring, draggle-tailed and dirty as you are."

"Your house?" Louisa's suspicions began to crystallize into an unpleasant certainty. "What kind of a house is this?"

"An expensive one." Her voice was filled with pride. "You won't find any poxy old whores here—just clean young girls eager to please a man with money in his pocket, the best food in the medina, and even a drop of wine for those inclined. It turns a pretty penny to keep me in my old age."

"You would have me lie with men for money?" She would rather die than be forced to spread her legs and let any man take her at his pleasure. "You want to make me into a whore?"

The old woman shook her head regretfully. "You'd be too much trouble to train, or I'd do just that. As it is, I'll sell you directly and let someone else have the job of taming you. You'd be an asset to any house, but now that I'm older I don't have the energy to break you in to the business. I'm guessing a wealthy Arab will be adding you to his harem before I'm much older. Lots of men are ready to pay well for a pretty blond concubine to train to give them pleasure."

While they were talking, she had led Louisa into a small room with a tiled floor that sloped down to a drain in the center. A row of buckets lined the wall under a couple of taps. The old woman turned the handle of a tap, filling one of the buckets with steaming water. "Come now, off with your clothes."

Louisa gazed at the water in the buckets with a desperate desire. Though she longed for both a drink and a bath, maybe it would be better if she stayed dirty. Surely no man would buy her for his harem in her sorry state. If they could not make a profit from her, they would have to let her go. She made no move to undress herself. "And if I do not wish to bathe?"

The old woman shrugged. "Then I will have you stripped and beaten, and you will bathe anyway." She turned away, muttering to herself. "Not to be touched. What nonsense. I will treat her as I treat any other slave girl."

Stripped and beaten for not wanting to wash herself? Louisa stepped backward in fright. What kind of place was this to threaten her with such a punishment?

"Do not look at me as if I had just eaten a child," the old woman snapped at her. "I have no patience with slaves who do not know their place. Now, get out of your clothes, or I shall summon the men to help. Some of them take particular delight in punishing unruly slave women."

Faced with the threat of force, Louisa hurriedly stripped down to her chemise and moved toward the buckets of water.

The old woman barred the way. "All your clothes," she demanded, looking with distaste at Louisa's shift. "You cannot bathe with your clothes on."

Louisa hesitated for a moment, but the woman's glower told her just how useless any protest would be. Shame reddening her cheeks, she lifted the shift over her head and, covering her nakedness with her hands as best she could, sat down on the cold, tiled floor.

The old woman's gaze softened a fraction. "That's more like it." She lathered up a washcloth with a soap that smelled of flowers, dipped it in the bucket of hot water, and attacked Louisa's body roughly, scrubbing her back and neck with vigor until her skin felt raw. "Now up you get, so I can wash the rest of you."

"I can wash myself," Louisa protested, holding out her hand for the washcloth.

"Not as well as I will wash you. Now get up, or I shall have to bring my helpers in."

Her face flaming, Louisa stood up naked on the tiled floor and allowed the woman to wash her down all over. The old woman allowed her no modesty at all, rubbing the soapy cloth over her breasts, under her arms, and even between her legs. "You've got a nice-looking body," she muttered approvingly, as she ran the cloth up and down Louisa's thighs and between her buttocks. "Young and firm flesh without any marks on it."

Louisa bit her lip at the indignity of it all, but she did not dare complain. The thought of a man being brought in to witness her humiliation was more than she could bear.

"It was a good day for me when the boys took you from the boat. You'll fetch me a few dinar when you're auctioned off tonight," the old woman continued, as she scrubbed. "But, pretty body notwithstanding, no one will buy a dirty slave girl."

Louisa stiffened. "Tonight?" She had hoped to have a few days to regain her strength of purpose—and to look for a way to escape, maybe even work on the conscience of her captor. Even such a hardened old rogue as this old brothel keeper must have a conscience hiding somewhere.

The old woman cackled, "Why delay and risk spoiling the merchandise?"

Her levity offended and insulted Louisa. Did the old bawd not care about the fate of all the women she had helped to sell into sexual slavery? "You auction off people all the time? Like cattle?" She did not understand how anyone could be so heartless.

"We do not have the big slave markets that we used to have when I was a girl. Then the boats would bring in scores of slaves at a time and line them up in the marketplace for sale— captured sailors for the most part. Some of the young ones, especially the ones with pretty golden hair, were worth every dirham I had to pay for them and more." She heaved a sigh as she rubbed soap into Louisa's hair, tugging on it unmercifully. "That was a sight to see. But nowadays slaves are a rare commodity and the auctions are small affairs, held indoors, away from prying eyes and tattling tongues. A pretty young girl like you will bring in the buyers from all around the Rif. They'll be looking to add an exotic touch to their harem. Now, rinse yourself off."

Louisa grabbed a bucket of hot water and tipped it over her head, as much to get the old woman's poisonous words out of her ears as to wash the soap off her hair. Another bucket of hot water rinsed the soap off the rest of her. She had to admit that it felt so good to be clean once more.

The old woman dried her roughly and gestured to a wooden bench in the corner. "Lie down over there."

Obediently, Louisa lay down on her stomach on the bench indicated. The old woman clapped her hands loudly and another young woman came in bearing a bottle of what looked like perfume. She stood over Louisa and dropped a trail of sweet-smelling oil on her back.

The old woman barked some instructions at her in a strange language and then left the two of them alone.

"Can you speak English?" Louisa whispered, but the other woman only murmured some words she could not understand, and began to smooth the oil into Louisa's back. Louisa tried to sit up, but the girl was stronger than she looked, and pushed her back down onto the bench. Another attempt at sitting up only earned her a quick slap across the buttocks that stung like nettles and a torrent of angry-sounding words. Defeated for the moment, she lay back quietly. This girl was clearly as disinclined to help her as the old woman.

She let her eyes drift shut as the girl's warm hands began to work the oil into her back, kneading it as if she were a lump of dough. Despite her best intentions, she could not help relaxing just a little. Though escape was first and foremost on her mind, it was difficult to keep focused while she was being massaged with such skill.

Before she had had half enough, the girl motioned for her to roll over. Reluctantly, Louisa rolled over onto her back, uncomfortable with her nudity in the presence of another woman. Since she had grown to be a woman, not even her sisters had seen her naked.

The girl took no notice of her blushes, but dropped some of the sweet-smelling oil onto her breasts and stomach, and proceeded to rub it into her skin as before. This time, her touch was less like a massage and more like a caress. The girl's hands lingered on her breasts, smoothing the scented oil over every inch of skin. Her nipples could not help but tighten at the touch.

The girl smoothed oil over her stomach in sweeping circular motions, and then, to Louisa's embarrassment, she dipped her hands between Louisa's legs and started to caress her intimately, smoothing over even her private parts with the scented oil. No one but Khair Bey had ever touched her there before. Louisa sat up with a cry and tried to push the girl's hands away, but her protest was no use.

At a call from the girl, two men strode into the room. They took in the situation with a leer, and knelt on either side of Louisa, holding her shoulders down with one hand. The girl continued to push Louisa's legs apart, spreading her wide open and teasing her with a few drops of oil dripped straight onto her private parts.

Louisa wanted to die of shame, but she could not move. All she could do was shut her eyes, shut out the sight of the men peering at her naked body and of the girl stroking her where no woman's hands had a right to be.

As the girl continued to dip her fingers in and out of the cleft between Louisa's legs, her body started to respond to the caresses. The oil was slick and the girl's caresses were skillful—at times light and teasing as the drop of a feather, and then strong and full of promise. She could feel herself getting wet and despite her shame, she pushed against the girl's hand, seeking more.

The girl responded by slipping one finger right inside her, making her moan with the pleasure of it. It was not right that a woman's caress should feel so good on her body, but there was no denying it. The air in the room seemed to grow ever hotter and more languid than ever, heavy with the smell of desire.

The men holding her felt it, too. They began to breathe heavily, and one of them reached over and touched a tight nipple with the back of his hand. She arched her back up to meet his touch, needing to the core what he wanted to give her, though her need shamed her. He laughed, a low guttural noise, and bent his head over her, flicking the tight bud with the tip of his tongue.

The man on the other side did likewise, kissing her breast as he continued to hold her down. Together they held her as their tongues licked at her breasts, leaving her no choice but to accept the caresses they forced on her.

Then all of the sudden, the girl withdrew her hand, leaving Louisa trembling on the brink of an orgasm. The men lifted their heads from her breasts and dropped their grip on her shoulders, allowing her to sit up once again. One of them winked at her before they both followed the girl out of the room, leaving her alone for the first time.

Shakily, she got to her feet and looked around for her clothes, for anything that would cover her naked body. She could feel that her face was hot with desire, and the wetness between her legs. If only they had kept caressing her for just a moment more, she would not have been left so desperate, absolutely trembling with the need for satisfaction.

She reached down and touched herself tentatively where the girl had caressed her. She only needed a little more, just a very little—maybe her own fingers would be enough.

Yes, it felt almost as good as before. Her fingers slipped easily between her legs, the oil making them slick. As her touch grew stronger and surer, her desperate desire started to rise once more.

Just as she started to feel herself approaching an orgasm once more, the old woman bustled in, and Louisa snatched her hand away, her face flaming, wiping the oil from her fingers onto her thigh. Her breasts felt heavy and the burn between her legs was almost unbearable.

The old woman looked at her with a knowing glint in her eye, but made no comment. "Here, make your hair tidy," she said, tossing her a wide-toothed comb.

She caught the comb with a sob of frustration. If only Khair Bey were here, he would not leave her in such a state of need. He would feed the fire that consumed her until he pushed her over the edge of pleasure, and then he would let her rest in his arms.

But Khair Bey was far away in Naples, and she would never

see him again, never hold him in her arms. Another man would buy her tonight and take her to his bed. Tonight a stranger would caress her breasts, slip his hands between her thighs, and thrust into her until he spent his seed. He would take her, roughly or gently as he pleased, and she would not be able to fight him off. And then she would be locked up in a harem for the rest of her life.

She wasn't sure which frightened her more—the thought of being forced into intimacy with a complete stranger who might mistreat her or hurt her, or the thought of being caged in a harem for years, maybe forever. What scared her was the lack of power, the freedom to choose a path for herself. Being at the mercy of another human being was a sure road to discontent, if not outright misery.

"And hurry along. Some of them are already growing impatient to see you."

She attacked the tangles in her hair with a vicious hand. Sitting here crying over her situation would not help matters. Maybe the man who bought her would be kind and set her free when he had tired of her. Not all men were cruel and perverse, or would take delight in hurting or humiliating her.

Maybe she would be lucky and find a man who could arouse her passions as Khair Bey did. Maybe he would be gentle and loving and treat her well. She gave a snort at her foolish optimism and tugged her hair until her scalp stung.

"Where are my clothes?" They were no longer on the floor where she had dropped them, and she was anxious to cover herself. When she was properly dressed once more it would be easier to forget how she had shamed herself with her need. Modesty and nakedness were uneasy bedfellows.

"Those old rags?" The old woman spat on the floor in disgust. "I had them taken away and burned while you bathed."

Tears pricked at her eyes. Losing her dress, even though it was old and drab, was the final blow to her spirits. Now she truly had nothing left of her old life. "Then what am I to wear?"

She was handed a loose robe of thin white silk, so sheer that the light shone right through it. Louisa stood there, simply holding it in her hands.

"Well, what are you waiting for?" the old woman demanded crossly. "Put it on."

She could not wear such an indecent gown, not when her whole body was still humming with desire. The flush on her chest, the telltale wet patch between her legs, even the peaking of her nipples would be seen right through it. "I have no undergarments."

"Undergarments? Rubbish. The men want to have a glimpse of what they are bidding for. You want to drive the price higher, not make them suspect you are hiding a deformity under your clothes. Now, put it on and hurry."

Louisa thrust her arms into the sleeves of the gown and buttoned it up across her chest. It hung loosely around her body, allowing the outlines of her limbs to be plainly seen through it. She hugged her arms tightly around herself to hide whatever she could. It was almost more indecent than being naked. "I cannot wear this. Truly, I cannot."

"Would you rather be whipped first? You *will* be auctioned tonight, even if I have to drag you there kicking and screaming myself. Though you are still a bit pale . . ." She pinched Louisa's cheeks roughly to make them pink. "There, you will do nicely. Your pretty face will speak for itself—it doesn't need any more primping."

Louisa's throat was dry with fear. "Can I have a glass of water?" Her thirst had been exacerbated by the bath and the heat of the room.

"There is no time. Do you think I have nothing better to do than to wait on you?" She hurried to the door and clapped her hands together loudly. The same pair of guards instantly appeared, their looks of hope replaced with disappointment at seeing Louisa no longer naked and at their mercy.

Louisa looked down at the floor, ashamed at her state of undress and even more so at the prickle of awareness between her thighs at the sight of them. The pair had handsome, strong bodies. She would like to have them both at her mercy, as she had been at theirs. She would tie them to the bench and stroke their cocks with her hands and mouth until they were as hard as the wood they were lying on. Then she would lower herself down onto first one and then the other, taking them inside her in turns, filling herself with their thickness . . .

The old woman addressed them in a rapid-fire torrent of foreign words. "As for you, young missy," she leaned in closer to Louisa, spittle flecking the corner of her mouth. "You will do as you are told, or you will suffer the consequences. Here in the Rif we have a way of dealing with naughty slaves that does not ruin their value. We give them the bastinado—we beat them on the soles of their feet until they faint from the pain. Believe me, you have never felt anything so exquisitely painful." She gave a twisted grimace. "It was two years before I could walk again after I was beaten."

Louisa shuddered with horror, all lustful thoughts temporarily forgotten, as she was led away by the guards. The gown swirled open as she walked, leaving nothing of her most private parts hidden at all. She felt even more naked for wearing such a pretense of clothing that only drew attention to her body rather than covered it.

It seemed her fate was to be sold as a slave to the highest bidder. If she resisted, she would be beaten on the soles of her feet until she couldn't walk, and then sold as a slave regardless.

A tear slid down her cheeks, but she could not even raise a hand to wipe it away. It was just as well that Khair Bey was not here to see her brought so low; she had rejected him so proudly just a few short days ago. Even a man as generous as he was would have to feel some tiny spark of gratification to see her so humbled.

The guards took her to a spacious chamber, filled with men lounging on low sofas, many of them smoking pipes. The air was so thick with tobacco fumes it made her eyes water, and she coughed to clear the smoke from her lungs.

At her entrance, the conversation gradually died away as all the men turned to stare at her.

Walking with tiny steps to keep her gown together, she was led to a raised platform in the center of the room. The guards dropped her arms and stood, one on either side of her, to prevent any hope of escape.

From the platform she could see every corner of the room, and she knew all eyes were fastened on her. There was nowhere for her to run, nowhere she could hide. In the indecent gown she was wearing, all of her was on display to anyone who cared to look. And all the men in the room were eyeing her avidly, as horse fanciers at a horse sale would eye up a particularly fine young mare they longed to break and ride.

She could feel their eyes on her as if they were a hundred hands crawling all over her body, touching her in every imaginable place. She shuddered with the humiliation of exposure, of being made to endure their stares as their gaze raked across her shoulders, roved over her breasts, and lingered on the tightness of her nipples and the moist triangle of hair at the juncture of her thighs.

As soon as she crossed her arms across her chest to conceal herself, the guards took hold of her hands and forced her to drop her arms to her sides again. Three times she tried before she was forced to acknowledge that she had to stand there without making any attempt to cover herself. Her helplessness only added to her humiliation.

By now she was beyond exhaustion and so thirsty she would almost have put herself up for sale in exchange for a glass of water. The heat in the room made her sweat and the smoke prickled uncomfortably on her skin. Nevertheless, she stood there as still as a statue, with tears of shame rolling down her hot cheeks. Only her fear kept her standing upright.

The noise in the room gradually picked up and became animated as the men on the sofas drew out their money pouches and waved them around excitedly in the air. The clamor grew to a crescendo when a man stepped onto the platform next to Louisa.

Before she realized what his intentions were, he had whipped off her transparent gown and was waving it above his head with a flourish. Utterly naked now, with nothing but her blushes to cover her, she gave a cry and dropped to her knees, only to be forced to her feet again by the guards. There they held her, one on each arm, displaying her to her would-be purchasers.

Dropping the gown onto the floor at his feet, the auctioneer began the bidding.

Six

With all pretense of casualness dropped now that her nakedness was on display, the men got to their feet and crowded around the platform. Some were clearly there to buy, adding their voices to the bidding, while others were more intent on ogling her nakedness than on permanently purchasing her.

One of the bolder ones even reached out and stroked her naked backside, but a swift blow from one of the guards sent him reeling to the back of the crowd. For the first time, she was glad of their presence beside her to keep the more raucous elements of the crowd away.

The bidding continued and the price drove higher. The number of active participants gradually decreased, as one by one the men were forced to drop out with a shouted curse or an angry mutter, depending on their level of disappointment.

She stared intently at the bidders around the room, knowing

that her future lay in the hands of the man who would pay the highest price for her tonight. A kindly man, she prayed, and one who would not treat her roughly—she dared not even pray for more.

Eventually, only two bidders were left. One of them was an effeminate young man in an embroidered coat, with smooth skin the color of ebony. She could not fathom what he might want with her. He seemed far more interested in caressing his male companion—a brown-skinned boy still too young to grow a beard—than he was in looking at her naked body. The pair of them whispered together and giggled in a high-pitched tone, bidding on her as if they were taking part in a wonderful joke.

The other man left in the race was a gargantuan beast with a heavy black beard, a fierce-looking knife at his belt, and a vicious look in his eyes. He reminded her of the fairy tale of Bluebeard, the man who had married and then murdered twenty women, one after the other. This man looked evil and threatening enough to be Bluebeard's brother.

When he wasn't staring at her greedily, he was throwing poisonous glances at the young man in the embroidered coat. She shuddered at the thought of belonging to the black-browed giant. He did not look like the kindly man she was hoping for. Even the others in the crowd had left a space around him, clearly fearing his temper and not daring to jostle him.

The bidding war between the two continued for some minutes until eventually the young man shrugged easily as if to say that the joke had gone far enough, and wandered off to the back of the crowd with his companion.

A triumphant grin split the face of the vicious-looking giant and he elbowed his way through the crowd to claim his prize. She closed her eyes in defeat. So, this man was to be her master? Brutality was then to be her bedfellow and cruelty her constant companion.

Oh, how she wished she had accepted Khair Bey's offer now. If she had to be locked away in a harem, better by far that it had been by him. He would at least have treated her as a woman—as his valued mistress, not as a slave. But it was too late for idle wishing. She had rejected him, and now fate was repaying her for it.

Just then she heard a door open behind her, and a hush came over the room. The voices quieted as if muffled in a blanket, and even the triumphant shouting of the black-bearded beast was hushed.

She twisted her head to see who had entered, and her shame was complete.

Khair Bey stood in the doorway, his face black with anger. Khair Bey, whom she had allowed to seduce her with his fine words, whom she had left rather than become one of his harem, was seeing her in all her degradation—naked and being auctioned off to a room full of strangers.

As much as she had wished to see him again, she had never wanted it to be like this. Even the hope of escape that he offered was nothing when compared to the awfulness of having him see her in such a state.

This last humiliation was too much for her to bear. Despite the guards stationed next to her, she sank to the floor, covered her face in her hands, and wept in agony.

This time, they did not pull her to her feet again, but allowed her to bury her ignominy and sorrow.

Through her storm of weeping, she heard a few harsh commands being barked out, and then some angry mutterings and shuffling as the room cleared out.

Even when she had run out of tears, and the room had fallen silent around her, she stayed collapsed on the floor. Maybe if she stayed like that for long enough, her nightmare would end and she would wake up home in England again, in her own bed.

A soft touch on her shoulder startled her. "Go away," she muttered into her arms. She had endured enough for one day. Even if they were to kill her on the spot for her disobedience, she could not take any more.

"Louisa." It was his voice—the voice of the man she had tried to escape; the man who had caused this whole sorry situation in the first place. "You are safe now."

She would have started crying again if she could produce any more tears to cry. "Go away."

He picked up the horrid gown and spread it over her, covering her nakedness. Then he picked her up and cradled her in his arms like an infant. "I have you. You are safe now."

She huddled into his arms, hiding her face as he carried her through the house and into the courtyard, where a litter carried by two porters waited. He placed her inside the litter, arranging the cushions under her head. Quietly, she allowed him to take charge. Whatever he did with her, her situation could not get any worse. "Where are you taking me?"

"Away from here."

She could not argue with that. She would go anywhere with him to get away from this house of horror.

The porters picked up the litter and carried it back into the streets. Peeking through the curtains, she saw Khair Bey striding in front, confident and proud. His closeness comforted her. Though he had been born in this savage land, he was not a cruel man. He had taken her away from the slave auction, rescuing her from a dreadful fate as the captive of Bluebeard. He would take care of her.

A few minutes later, she found herself ushered into a set of airy apartments owned by a friend of Khair Bey's. Seeing Louisa's disheveled state, their host brought them a pot of tea and some honey cakes, and tactfully left them alone.

She could hug Khair Bey for saving her, but she didn't dare. They had not exactly parted as friends and she felt awkward with the new man she saw in front of her. In his homeland, he seemed to stand even prouder than ever, with an air of remoteness he had not possessed in Italy. Now that they were on his home ground, she felt his power and influence as she had never felt it before. In Italy he had been one more rich merchant among many others, but here in Morocco, he was truly a prince.

Seated on a low couch in the private salon with the gown wrapped tightly around her body and her legs tucked to one side, she cradled a cup of mint tea in her hands and took a series of huge gulps. It burned all the way down, but she hardly cared. Her head hurt and her tongue was still thick with thirst. She could drink the ocean dry and still not be satisfied. "They were going to sell me."

He refilled her cup, adding a splash from a pitcher of cold water. "I know. I will have the woman punished for treating you so roughly."

The now lukewarm mint tea tasted quite different from the Earl Grey she had been used to drinking in the Winterbottoms' household. She finished her second cup and held it out for more. Though it was sweeter than she preferred, on the whole it didn't taste too bad, and it was wonderfully refreshing. Already she was starting to feel better. "How did you know I was there?"

"After you left Italy, I returned here to Morocco. I had only just arrived in port and was seeing to business when I heard that some buccaneers were selling a pretty young English girl, as if it were fifty years ago and slavery was still common around these parts. I was curious, and frankly concerned that my home country would still be involved in such barbarism as kidnapping and selling innocent women. I used my influence and had the sale stopped. You might say I rescued you."

Louisa felt completely confused, her thoughts in disarray from what she had been through. "So I am free then? Free to continue my journey home?"

He was looking at her as if she were a silly child who refused to see what was in front of her. "You belong to me. You became mine in Italy, and you doubly became mine when I rescued you. You will come with me to my home."

The mint tea suddenly seemed cloying. He had not changed so very much. He still wanted her to bow down in servitude to him, to acknowledge his superiority over her. She could never do that and remain true to herself. That was why she could not have stayed with him.

As much as she had yearned for him since she had left Italy, it took only a few minutes in his company to remind her of why she had been forced to leave. Though she longed for his touch and wanted nothing more than to curl up in his arms and feel safe from the world, she could never be happy with a man like him. He would never let her be herself.

Despite the trouble that had led from her decision to leave, it had been the right one, she was surer of that now than ever. "I am an Englishwoman. I belong to no one." He was a danger to her peace of mind, to her sense of self. If she stayed with him, he would swallow her up into him, until there was nothing left of Louisa. She *had* to learn to live without him.

He cradled his own cup of tea in his hands as if it were as fragile as her heart. "I'm afraid that isn't quite correct. Slavery is still perfectly legal here, though the abduction of Europeans is frowned upon because we do not wish to give the Spaniards or the French any excuse to make war with us again. But by the laws of this country, you belong to me now."

The true meaning of the abrupt stop to the auction suddenly became clear. "You bought me?" How could she have been so blind not to see it before now? Of course money must have changed hands—lots of it, too. The venal old woman who had bathed her would never have let him simply take her, not when the old bawd was counting on a tidy profit to come her way from her trade in human flesh.

"I did."

"To be your slave? Not to set me free?"

He leaned back on one elbow on the embroidered floor cushions. "Slave is such a harsh word. You belonged to me the night you first accepted me into your bed. I have merely formalized the relationship between us. Now you belong to me in every way a woman can belong to a man."

To have freedom snatched away from her when it had been so close—it was worse than despair. "You cannot own me."

"You gave yourself to me of your own volition. When you were in trouble, I rescued you. Now I must protect you."

"I do not want your protection. I never asked for it. Set me free. Let me go to England as I wanted." If she could work on his conscience to free her—if he let her go—all might not yet be lost.

He looked almost sorry to refuse her. "It is too late for that. You belong with me now."

If he did not see how hateful this seemed to her, he did not understand her. He would never understand her. "How could you?" Her voice was a whisper of pain.

An indignant look crossed his face. "Would you rather I had abandoned you to take your chances with a stranger? Baqir El Kamche, the man who was prepared to pay the highest price for you before I doubled his offer and forced him to cede, is well-known for beating his slaves to death if they displease him. Would you rather be owned by such a beast? To lie with him in his bed every night, to suffer his lips kissing you and his coarse hands on your body—hands that were still bloody from beating his previous bed partner until she was dying from it? Would you have such a man roughly take his pleasure with you night after night, with no thought or care for what you needed in return? And for him to beat you, too, when he was tired of you?"

"It would be less of a betrayal." Being bought by such a man would disgust her to the very marrow, but it could not hurt as much as being a slave to her former lover. It would not rip her heart into little pieces. Khair Bey knew how much she valued her freedom. If he cared for her at all, he would set her free and let her make her own choice.

He dismissed her pain. "You are not thinking straight. You should be on your knees thanking me for saving you."

She looked him straight in the eyes. "Are you going to set me free and take me back to England?"

"No, you belong with me." The finality in his voice told her all she needed to know.

"Then you bought me for your own purposes, not for mine." She turned her head away so he could not read the desolation in her face. "I see no need to thank you."

"I could have you beaten for your insolence, you know," he said idly, as he lounged back on the cushions. "No one would think it unusual if I were to correct an unruly slave."

"You will beat me on the soles of my feet until I cannot walk?" Her voice dripped with all the disgust she felt at such a barbaric practice. "How cultured and sophisticated of you."

"Come now, Louisa. I was teasing you. I would not beat you."

"I suppose you want me to thank you for that, as well." Her voice dripped sarcasm.

"That would be preferable to being hissed at by an angry kitten."

The fight suddenly drained out of her. Nothing she could say or do seemed to get through to him. He did not see her as a woman, but as a toy, a child, a kitten. It was as if they did not even speak the same language. "I'm tired," she said abruptly. She needed to get away from him before she lost her self-control and started to rave and scream like a madwoman.

"Forgive me," he replied, urbanely courteous once more. "You have had a trying day. Let me show you to your room." He rose from his lounging position on the floor and led the way to a sumptuous room decorated richly in red and gold. In the center of the room stood a bed with wrought iron ends, covered in a finely woven bedspread that looked as soft as gossamer. Red patterned carpets were scattered on the mosaic tiled floor, and even the plaster ceiling was carved into intricate designs.

She sucked in her breath. Never had she seen such luxury in all her life, not even in the houses of the Winterbottoms' most wealthy friends. "These are the slave quarters?"

"These are the quarters that my favorite slave has been invited to share with her master," he replied.

She knew why he had bought her, but hearing it stated so boldly made her want to weep. In Italy, he had offered to marry her and she had turned him down. Now that he no longer needed to wed her to ensure her presence in his bed, it seemed she was to be his mistress, his concubine until he tired of her. She was no longer worthy of marriage. The prospect made her feel depressed to the bone. Captive or not, she was in no mood to pander to his desires. "I am tired," she repeated. Would he sell her off to some other man when he wearied of her, or simply throw her out onto the street like a broken toy?

To her surprise, he merely bowed. "Good night." And just like that, she was alone.

She padded around the room, examining her gilded prison. It was the most beautiful room she had ever seen. She had always loved the carpets that Mr. Winterbottom traded, but she could tell at a glance that these were much finer than any he had ever brought home to show his wife. These were as soft as down on her bare feet—and so fine they had to be worth a king's ransom.

Khair Bey must have wealthy and influential friends indeed, if they could live in such luxury.

She padded over to the bed. Given the heat of the climate, it had little in the way of bed coverings, but the sheets were of pure, smooth silk. She ran her hands over the fabric. She had never even owned a silk dress that she could remember, let alone slept on silk sheets. They seemed the most extravagant luxury she could ever imagine.

She had nothing to sleep in but the transparent gown she had been given by the old bawd, and which she never wanted to see again. Tired as she was, sleep would never come if she remained wrapped in that nasty thing. With a grimace of distaste, she threw it off her shoulders and let it drop to the floor in a heap. Then, scuttling as quickly as she could, she clambered in between the sheets and pulled the covers over her.

The silk sheets were as cool as a glass of iced water on her skin, and a light breeze came in from the open window to ruffle the heat of the evening. Her eyes drifted shut.

She barely had the time to worry about what would happen if Khair Bey changed his mind about sharing her quarters before she was fast asleep.

Khair Bey stood and watched the woman sleeping in his bed. Her reactions today had puzzled him. Surely any young woman captured by Barbary pirates and about to be sold as a slave to the highest bidder—a man who looked as ferocious and unkempt as a bear—would be glad to be rescued. Why wasn't she on her knees thanking him for his timely rescue, as he had expected?

She did not know that he had orchestrated it all, that it was his men who had captured her boat and terrified the captain into giving her up. He was positive she had not seen him on the deck, watching her, as she was brought to his ship. It was his men who had taken her to the brothel and arranged with the old bawd for her to be sold at auction for a cut of the profit. The brothel keeper had not known that he was behind her pretty acquisition—she could have told no tales on him. And, finally, he had turned up and bought Louisa himself, rescuing her from what must have seemed like hell on earth.

There was no way she could have known that he had engineered the situation. She spoke no Berber, and none of his men spoke more than a couple of words of English—certainly not enough for them to give away his involvement in the affair.

Instead of being thankful, though, she had attacked him as if she knew he had been the cause of her distress.

He ruthlessly squelched the pang of guilt he felt at the lines of worry on her face—lines that not even sleep had erased. She was here in Morocco where she belonged. Though she had not come of her own free will, she was here nonetheless. He would not feel guilty for bringing her to his homeland to be with him. It was where she belonged.

From now on, her life would be one of ease and luxury. She would not have to toil as a servant in another woman's house. She would have her own house and servants to attend to her. Never would she regret that she had become his woman.

He slipped out of his clothing and lay on the bed next to her, drawing the covers over them both. Though she was asleep, he could not resist running his hand softly over her rounded hip and thigh. No woman was more beautiful in his eyes than she. She stirred at his touch but, in her exhaustion, did not wake.

His own body leaped to life at her nearness, but he ignored its call. He would not take her now, not when she was tired and overwrought with the strain of acclimatizing to a new country. When he next made love to her, it would be because she begged him to, because she wanted his touch and craved having him inside her, making her whole. She would be an eager participant in their lovemaking, not merely a passive recipient of his attentions.

Seducing her into his arms again would be a challenge, but one that he would relish. He wanted this woman with every breath he took. In his eyes, she had belonged to him from the moment she first kissed him. He had to make her see what was crystal clear to him—that she would be his forever.

Khair Bey was lounging in an armchair, just watching her, when Louisa awoke the next morning. "I have been to the souk   the market—this morning," he announced.

She cowered under her bedclothes, uncomfortably aware of her nakedness. If he were to join her this morning, his naked body in the bed next to her own, she was not sure she would have the strength to resist him. Even sitting at his ease in the chair, he exuded a powerful sensuality that had her prickling with awareness. She clutched the sheet tighter to hide the peaking of her nipples. Now that he thought she belonged to him, she had to keep him at an even greater distance than before. Giving in to her attraction to him would spell the beginning of the end for her.

Khair Bey seemed amused at her shyness. "Come now, Louisa, where do you think I slept last night?"

She looked around the room, but could see no pallet on the floor, or any indication that he had shared the room with her.

"You were fast asleep when I joined you in the bed. You did not so much as twitch in your sleep all night."

"You shared the bed with me?" She glared at him, hating the thought of him seeing her vulnerable in her sleep. Didn't he respect any boundaries?

"These are my quarters, after all, and you are lying in my bed. Where else am I to sleep?"

Her near orgasm at the hands of the massage girl the previous evening was starting to affect her now. She should have stroked herself more quickly and relieved her need before being interrupted by the old bawd. If she had found satisfaction yesterday, she would not be so hot between her legs right now at the thought of having slept next to Khair Bey all night. "Then give me a space of my own. One that I am not expected to share with you." Half of her wished he would simply ignore her protests, strip the bedclothes off her naked body, and make love to her right away. Her mouth watered at the prospect, even though she knew she had to resist the temptation.

He waved an arm around the room. "You would give up all this luxury for a cupboard under the stairs?"

"I don't need silk sheets and beautiful carpets. I would give up everything for my freedom." Or for the touch of his hands on her breasts and between her legs, stroking her until she cried out with pleasure in his arms.

"I am glad you think the carpets are beautiful. They are woven by my people. We are proud of our skill at the loom."

"You won't let me go, will you?"

"My people are Berbers. We live mostly in the mountains and foothills of Morocco. We shall travel there today, to my house in the country, if you feel up to the journey."

She did not want to go anywhere. What she really wanted was to stay in bed and have him overpower her and take her, even though she struggled and fought him. That way, she could enjoy the pleasure he would bring her without suffering the guilt of having given in. "Do I have a choice?"

"You always have a choice."

"Then take me to England. That is the only choice I want to make." However much she wanted to make it the truth, to her shame it was a lie. She wanted to give in to her desires and stay with him almost as much as she wanted to leave.

"England is a cold, gray place, or so I have heard. You would never be happy there. But even though England is out of the question, you still have a choice. You can choose to leave for the foothills today, or stay here for another night and rest. The journey is not a long one, but I will understand if you do not feel up to making it just yet."

She shrugged and turned her head away so he could not read her desire for him in her eyes. "What do I care?" Her resistance was perilously close to slipping and she had to fight to keep it in place.

"Come, Louisa, there is no need to sulk." She felt the bed sink next to her as he came and sat beside her, but she did not turn to look at him. "I have bought you some new clothes at the market."

Did he expect her thanks for providing her with a basic necessity? It was not her fault that she came to him with nothing, without even a dress to wear. "I suppose you want my thanks for that, too."

He lifted his eyebrows expectantly.

"I see no reason to be particularly grateful. Your choice was either to provide me with something to wear or leave me naked all day long."

"Now *there's* a good idea. I wonder why I did not think of it myself."

The desire in his voice made her stomach turn over in knots. It reminded her all too clearly that she was in his power now, and if he chose to let her remain naked all day, she could do little about it. As a free woman with the ability to choose her course of action, she had found his presence unsettling, enticing, and even irresistible. As his captive, she ought to wish only for a chance to escape.

Freedom, independence, partnership—they might be nothing more than ideas, but they had always been important to her. She could not conceive of a future without them.

A cruel twist of fate had sent her into the arms of the man she craved above all others—the man who would enslave her and bend her to his will, until there was nothing left of Louisa. She could not reconcile her two desires; they would tear her apart.

Though she wanted to be his lover, she did not want to be his concubine, an inmate of his harem. She wanted to be herself. If she was not free to be Louisa, she might as well be dead. "Leave me some privacy, and I shall dress myself." She needed space to herself, to get out of his company for just a short while. It was easier to muster her defenses against him when he wasn't in front of her looking so enticing. "We may as well leave today as linger here another night."

She'd still been in shock last night when she had been brought here, and had seen nothing of the town or its environs. She wasn't even sure which way she would need to head to reach the sea. Leaving the house would give her a chance to scout out the territory and plan her next move. Once they were on the road, she could determine what she had to deal with and draw up her plans accordingly. For despite her desire for him, she would surely escape.

"Your wish is my command." With a polite bow, he turned on his heel and left her.

As much as she wanted to bury her head in the pillows and pretend this whole nightmare was not happening, she could not cower in bed all day. As soon as she was sure he had gone, she crawled out of bed and headed for the pile of clothes he had left behind.

Lingerie like she had never seen before was heaped on the carpet—fine lawn, silk, and even a few pieces in smooth satin. She put her hands into the middle of the pile, luxuriating in its touch as it glided against her skin. As a nursery maid, she could never afford such beautiful things to wear next to her skin. They were out of reach, even in her dreams.

It was wrong to be seduced by such frippery, but really, she could not help loving the feel of silk against her body. He need never know the delight she took in wearing his gifts, or he would surely try to turn it to his advantage.

Fearing that he would be back at any moment and catch her at a disadvantage, she washed herself hurriedly with the pitcher of warm water left for the purpose, and chose some undergarments almost at random. They slithered on as cool as water, and so light that it felt almost as if she was wearing nothing at all.

A long skirt of fine, sky blue wool came next, with a surprisingly modest embroidered white cotton bodice to match, and she was dressed. Though the style differed from what she was used to wearing, the fabric was soft and comfortable. She was glad he had indulged his taste for luxury only in her undergarments, and bought her sensible, workaday clothes to wear on top. Modest and practical, and free of any unnecessary ornamentation, they were the sort of clothes she was used to wearing, though certainly of a vastly superior quality to what she could buy for herself.

She'd expected something frivolous and impractical, the sort of expensive clothes a man would dress his mistress in, proclaiming to the world that she was a kept woman. Such clothes would have shamed her. To his credit, he had understood that much about her.

She smoothed her palms over her skirts, telling herself fiercely that she was in charge, in control of her destiny. She was not as weak and vulnerable as Khair Bey thought she was. Her strength to endure whatever he could throw at her would be her greatest weapon.

By the time the door opened to readmit him, she was as ready as she could be to face him—and her future.

Khair Bey tucked a red and white striped shawl around Louisa's shoulders. "There now, you look like a proper Berber woman." His heart ached with pride to see how beautiful she looked in the dress of his homeland. As his wife, she would do him much honor. Not even the most antagonistic village elder could find fault with her appearance this morning. She wore the clothes of a Berber woman with grace and dignity.

Taking her by the hand, he led her over to a chestnut mare

he had purchased especially for her use. "Meet Zahra. She will carry you to my riad in the Rif. We have a long ride ahead of us, but, God willing, we should be there by sundown."

Louisa put out one tentative hand and stroked Zahra on her nose. The mare whickered softly at the attention. "I had thought we would be taking a carriage," she said hesitantly. "I have not ridden a horse before."

He picked her up and set her on the mare's back, stifling a smile at the look of alarm that passed over her face as she found herself perched so high. "The roads hereabouts are too narrow and rutted for even the lightest carriage. Horses and donkeys are better suited to this rocky terrain than carriages. In the south, where the desert sands lie, we ride camels. And Zahra has a gentle gait."

His words had clearly not reassured her. She was holding on to the pommel of the saddle so tightly that her knuckles had turned white. "I hope so," she muttered. "Or I fear I shall fall off and be relegated to riding a donkey."

Her lack of experience on a horse was clear. She sat on the mare as if she were a sack of grain, rather than moving with the motion of the animal. She looked stiff and uncomfortable and very ill at ease.

No matter; he would teach her to ride as well as any Moroccan woman. He swung his legs over the back of his own horse, took the mare's bridle to lead her, and motioned to their escorts to follow. The men would provide protection for them on the journey, and their donkeys would carry the goods he had promised to bring back to his people, the goods he had purchased with some of the profits from the sale of their carpets. His time in Italy had been well spent, in more ways than one.

As soon as they left the seaside town behind and were into the open air of the countryside amid the groves of almond trees that covered the rocky ground, he felt his breathing deepen. This was where he belonged, where he felt truly alive. He did not feel at home in the warehouses of Italy, haggling over the price of carpets. His heart, his soul, was bound to the earth of the Rif, the mountains and plains of Morocco.

If Louisa would come to love his country as much as he, then he would ask for nothing more.

He turned around to watch her. Her initial trepidation at the unfamiliar sensation of riding a horse had given way to a much greater sense of ease. Her death grip on the saddle had lessened, and she no longer drew her breath in sharply when the mare stumbled slightly on the rough road. Now she was looking around her with wide eyes, no longer fixated on the road at her feet, but drinking in the surrounding view.

Even though he had grown up here and knew every hill and valley like the back of his hand, the beauty of the landscape still had the power to take his breath away.

In the far distance, high mountains capped with snow dominated the horizon, while behind them lay the sea spread out like a bright blue carpet as far as the eye could see. The road, little more than a rutted track, wended its way upward over man-made terraces thickly planted in durum wheat and olive trees. On the higher slopes, small flocks of goats grazed on the grassy banks hidden among the rocks.

Louisa's voice broke in on his thoughts. "How far are we going?"

He pointed toward the low range of hills in front of them. "Behind those hills lies a beautiful, fertile valley. That is where my casbah lies."

"Your casbah? What is that?"

"My village. A casbah is a walled village."

A puzzled look crossed her face. "Why does a simple village need walls?"

"Morocco is a beautiful land, with many rivers and lush valleys. Many people covet it, from the Arabs to the French. Our village walls have helped to keep my Berber people safe from centuries of invaders who envied our lands."

She was silent for a moment, digesting his answers. "And what is your house like, in this walled village?"

"It is just a house as any other house. Men's quarters, women's quarters, a rooftop terrace for the warm summer evenings. But it has a large courtyard and beautiful gardens planted with flowers and set with fountains," he said proudly. "The water plays all day, cooling the air even in the heat of summer." The gardens were a symbol of his prosperity, and of the wealth of his people. His lands were fertile and well tended, and afforded him luxuries that others who cared less for their land could not match. "You will like it there."

"Who lives there with you?"

"In my village?"

"In your house."

"My mother, several aunts—the sisters of my late father—some other relatives, and various servants who look after us all. We are not a large group. There are maybe a dozen of us altogether."

"Do you have other women like me?" She stumbled a little over the words. "Other women you have bought?"

"No, I do not." Though slavery was still commonplace in other parts of Morocco, he had never condoned the practice in the lands he controlled. His capture of Louisa had been an aberration, and the sultan would doubtless have his head for piracy and abduction if word of it ever got out. Capturing European women was the one action calculated to bring the wrath of the European powers onto the heads of all Moroccans, and it was swiftly and brutally punished.

"What about the fifty women in your harem? I cannot believe they all remain there of their own free will. Are none of them captives? And if they do not live with you, where do they live?"

He gave a bark of laughter. "Whatever gave you the idea that I had a harem of slave girls?"

"You told me so . . . in Italy."

He shook his head. She must have mistaken his teasing for the truth. Only the sultan himself would lead such a profligate life, and keep so many women to underscore his own status.

"What on earth would I do with fifty women? How would I keep them? I am a wealthy man, but even my wealth has limits. I would not choose to squander my family's property and honor on such foolishness. Fifty concubines?" And he burst out laughing again at the thought.

Louisa's bottom lip trembled. "You told me you had at least fifty women in your harem and I believed you. Why shouldn't I? Everyone knows that Arabs keep hundreds of women as their wives, all locked away together in a prison. How was I to know that you would be any different?"

He would almost be offended by her questions if he was not so amused by them. "I am a Berber. We do not keep harems of wives like our Arab brothers, nor do we have more than one wife."

She was silent for some moments. "I didn't know you were joking. I thought you were all the same, and lived in the same way."

"There is much you do not know about life in Morocco. But you will learn."

In the early afternoon, they stopped by the side of a stream to eat. Louisa flopped under the shade of a tree with a sigh and closed her eyes. Riding all morning had clearly tired her.

He passed her a small, flat loaf of bread stuffed with couscous and spiced lamb, and a handful of dates. "Eat." Though she had slept like the dead the night before, there were still dark shadows under her eyes and she looked more fragile than she had in Italy. He would need to be sure she ate well and did not tire herself. His English rose needed to be well tended to take proper root in a foreign soil.

When she had finished eating, she lay back down in the shade, grimacing as her backside came into contact with the ground. Clearly she had not exaggerated her lack of experience on a horse. She would be sore on the morrow.

There was little time for resting, though. If they were to reach the casbah before nightfall, they could not afford to linger long. Hyenas and jackals were common enough hereabouts to make spending the night out in the open less than wise—not to mention the odd pride of lions.

Large caravans found safety in numbers and in keeping a fire burning all night, but they were only a small party and vulnerable to the predators that lurked on the plains. Besides, he wanted to introduce Louisa to her new home while it was still light enough to see.

With some reluctance, he shook her awake. "Come, we must go."

Stiffly, she got to her feet and allowed him to lift her back onto the mare with only a slight grimace. "Is it far to go?"

"Not so far. We will be there before the sky grows dark."

The mare started off with a whinny, picking her way surefootedly over the stony ground, closely followed by his stallion, sidestepping with energy and good spirits. The load-bearing donkeys ambled slowly in their wake, stopping every now and then to grab a mouthful of greenery and conversing among themselves with hee-hawing cries.

Captive

It was late afternoon when they passed the crest of the hill and could look down into the valley at the walled village he called home. The fortifications of earth that surrounded it gleamed an orangey red in the sunshine, reflecting a golden warmth onto the white walls of the buildings within. From this height, only the thatched roofs of many of the houses could be seen, but his own house stood out, tall and bright in the late sun.

He stopped his horse with a slight pressure on the reins and stood looking down on his village. His heart swelled with the joy of returning to his home, and with the knowledge that he had brought back the woman of his dreams to share it with him. "My home, and yours."

Louisa merely looked at it with a disturbing lack of interest and shrugged her shoulders. "Your home, my prison."

Her words chilled him to his soul. He had not thought she would be so upset at being brought to his village. He needed her to fall in love with him so she no longer wanted to depart. Once she was safely installed in his home and could not easily choose another life, he would have to confess that he had been behind her abduction. Only then could he reward her with the knowledge he had captured her out of love, and that in truth she had never been his slave.

The closer they got to the casbah, the quieter Louisa grew, until her silence seemed to enclose her in a thick blanket that was impenetrable. No matter how he coaxed her, she would not talk to him. She did not even seem to hear him when he spoke to her.

No doubt the first sight of her new home had overwhelmed her, just as he had been surprised and startled at his first view of a European city built of colorless, soulless gray stone. With time, she would get accustomed to her new place in the world. He dared not believe her silence came from anything more sinister. He needed her love too much.

His mother was in the courtyard to greet him when they arrived. She enveloped him in her arms as he slid off the back of his horse, thankful to be done with the day's riding. "Ithry, I am glad you are home," she said in Berber.

He replied in the same language. "It is good to be here. I have missed my family and my home. But my business in Italy is concluded for the year, and my people will be pleased with the price I obtained for them. This year will be another prosperous one."

His mother's glance sidled over to Louisa, who was stiffly attempting to dismount from her mare. "I see you have brought us a guest."

He hurried over to lift Louisa down from her horse and escort her over to his mother. "Not a guest. I have brought home a wife," he said, still in Berber.

His mother's eyes grew wide and she frankly stared at the pair of them. "You are married?"

"Not yet," he confessed. "But we will be soon. She belongs to me."

Her eagle eyes searched Louisa's face, and she seemed to be happy with what she saw. "She is a lucky woman, to be the one you have chosen as your wife."

He bowed his head in agreement, not sure yet whether Louisa would entirely agree with his mother's assessment. "Louisa, this is my mother, Layla," he said in English. "Mother, this is Louisa Clemens."

His mother bowed her head politely. "You are very welcome to my son's house," she said, in English this time.

To his surprise, Louisa had gone as white as milk at the mention of his mother's name. "You should not introduce me to your family," she hissed at him in an undertone. "You are mocking me, and shaming yourself."

He shook his head. What was the matter with Louisa now?

"You bought me," she continued in a low whisper. "I am less than a servant. I am your . . . your . . ." Her voice tailed off as if she could not bear to put into words what she thought she was. "You should never have brought me here. No respectable woman can talk to me now, especially not your mother."

He brushed aside her concerns. "My mother does not care about such trifles and neither should you." They would be married soon, and all would be set right. Until then, she was a part of his family, whether she liked it or not.

"She ought to care. As I do. I cannot look her in the eyes."

"Nonsense . . ." he started to say, but was interrupted by his mother, who came forward and took Louisa's hand.

"You look tired from your journey," she said, drawing Louisa away from him and bringing their whispered argument to an end. "Come with me and I shall show you to the women's quarters. My son is good to us womenfolk. We have the best apartments in the whole of the riad. They face north, away from the sun, and stay quite cool even in the hottest weather, and the scent from the orange trees planted below the windows is quite delicious . . ."

As Louisa gave one last agonizing look over her shoulder at Khair Bey, his mother led her away and into the house, still chattering like a robin.

Seven

Louisa folded her arms around her stomach in discomfort as Khair Bey's mother led her through a pretty tiled courtyard and into a set of spacious apartments. The rooms here were light and airy, with tiled floors and windows opened to keep a cool breeze flowing through. After riding all day in the heat of the sun, coming inside was like a long, cold drink of water to her senses.

Khair Bey's mother fluttered around her, showing her to a low sofa and placing cushions behind her back. "I do apologize for not having the rooms ready to receive you. My son did not see fit to inform me that he was bringing home a guest. I will have the girls see to it right away. I am sure you would like to freshen up after your journey. It is such a long and tiring ride from the coast."

Louisa could not allow Khair Bey's mother to go on thinking that she was an honored visitor. "I should not be sitting here," she mumbled with embarrassment. "And you should not be waiting on me. I am not exactly a guest."

Khair Bey's mother looked up with mild curiosity as she poured Louisa a cup of mint tea. "You are not?"

"I am not here by choice. I was on my way back to England when my ship was captured by pirates and I was taken captive and sold. Khair Bey bought me," she could hardly force the hateful words through her lips, "from a brothel."

The shock on his mother's face at her story told Louisa everything she needed to know. Khair Bey had been wrong. His mother *did* care about such things. Louisa bit her lip to hold back tears of self-pity.

But when Khair Bey's mother spoke, her voice was soft and comforting, not harsh with accusation. "You were working there? Forgive me for saying so, but I cannot imagine my son bringing home the type of woman one would find in a place like that." She shook her head with some vigor and continued pouring the tea. "He has always had too much pride to come second to another man."

At least she could honestly defend herself from the charge of being a prostitute. "No, I was sold mere moments after I arrived. The owner said I was more trouble than I was worth to train to the trade, or she would have kept me herself." Thank heaven she had at least escaped that fate.

His mother's eyes narrowed as she sat back on a sofa opposite Louisa and sipped from her cup. "You are a virgin, then?"

Louisa choked on a mouthful of hot tea. Khair Bey's

mother clearly was not one to mince words, even about the most private of matters. She felt her face slowly start to burn red hot with shame. She wished the ground would open up and swallow her whole. Death would be preferable to the embarrassment she felt at having to explain herself.

"Not a virgin, either. I had met your son before, in Italy." Though she could not lie, neither could she say anything more if her life depended on it. To have to confess her weakness to Khair Bey's mother was the greatest mortification she could ever face. She could not bear it if the older woman thought badly of her.

"No matter." She brushed off Louisa's confession as if it were a trivial matter. "My son has brought you to his home, and I would be shamed if I treated you as less than an honored visitor." She clapped her hands and a servant girl entered. She gave a series of orders in a soft-sounding language and waved the servant away again to do her bidding. "Fatima will have the best apartment made up for you as soon as possible. But until then, come and meet the rest of our family."

Louisa allowed herself to breathe again, thankful she would not be treated with scorn and disgust. Khair Bey's mother was treating her better than she deserved, far better than she had expected. Maybe it was just the Moroccan way to be so gracious to a woman who, in English society, would be openly derided. Whatever the reason, she was grateful for it.

Khair Bey's mother—Layla, as she instructed Louisa to call her—took her through the women's apartments and introduced her to the women who lived there. A couple of very elderly aunts who dressed identically in loose gowns nodded and smiled toothlessly at her, not knowing a word of English. Their faces were heavily tattooed with blue dye—small circles on their cheekbones, dots over their eyebrows, and an intricate series of lines covering their chins.

Several other women of indeterminate middle age, with the same markings on their chins, were introduced as Layla's cousins. There was not a dancing girl in sight—not a single woman who could possibly be a rival for Khair Bey's affections. Nor were there any locks on the doors, or any indication that the women were not free to come and go as they pleased.

As hard as it was for her to comprehend, he must have been telling the truth when he said he had no harem. She'd been so sure that if she came to Morocco, she would have to share Khair Bey with other women. That, more than anything else, had made her decide to leave Italy before she could be tempted to carry on their affair. Living like that—even if she had been chief among them, as his only wife in the midst of a sea of concubines—would have killed her soul.

Though he had bought her from the old bawd, he had not treated her as a slave. Last night they had shared his living quarters, but he had made no move to touch her against her will, and he had bought her respectable clothes and brought her home to his family. Even his mother had treated her kindly.

Maybe, just maybe, Morocco would not be as bad a place as she had feared. Even the climate was not as fierce as she had expected. The air was warm and dry like it was in Italy, and she loved the heat and the sunshine.

If Khair Bey were to repeat his offer to marry her, and give her the choice whether to stay or to go, she could almost imagine choosing to stay here with him.

After settling into her sumptuous new apartment, Louisa was led by a young maid to the rooftop terrace where the other women had congregated in the last of the afternoon sun.

Gingerly, she lowered herself onto a pile of cushions and accepted yet another cup of mint tea. The other women welcomed her with smiles and gestures, while Layla translated scraps of their conversation as best she could.

Louisa was just feeling comfortably settled when the bell at the entryway to the women's apartments gave a loud peal. Layla waved a hand at one of the servants to answer it. She returned a few moments later and whispered her message in Layla's ear.

"Khair Bey respectfully requests the company of Louisa Clemens to dine with him this evening," Layla translated, her eyebrows raised. "What say you, Louisa? Do you wish to dine with my scapegrace son this evening? Or shall you send him your excuses and dine quietly with us instead?"

Louisa looked into the bottom of her cup of tea, and gave the clear, amber liquid a swirl. "Do I really have a choice?" she asked quietly. A soft breeze was blowing over the terrace and the air smelled of warmed earth. If only her muscles were not screaming in pain from the stiffness of being in the saddle all day, she would think she was in paradise.

"While you live in this riad, in the apartments of which I am the mistress, you will always have a choice." Layla's voice was firm.

"But if I refuse, can he not come in here and force me to accompany him?"

Layla made a horrified noise at the thought, and shook her head emphatically. "These are the women's quarters. He may not enter past the outer rooms we use to entertain guests—not even if he were invited in, which he never would be. He is a man. He has his own apartments, the courtyard, and the galleries for entertaining his guests. This part of the riad belongs to us."

So, the women's quarters were isolated from the rest of the household to keep the men out, not to keep the women in? This made Louisa regard her companions in a whole new light. "He cannot come in here at all?"

"Never."

"Or send someone to fetch me out?"

Layla gave an evil smile. "I would like to see him try."

Louisa took another sip of tea. It seemed somehow sweeter and more delectable than it had just a moment before. Truly, life in Morocco held endless surprises. The women had their own apartments where the men were not allowed to enter. If they chose to, they could live there unmolested, in peace and privacy. It was not locks on their doors that kept the women inside their quarters, but their own choice to remain secluded.

She was a foreigner here, though, and a slave. Although the system might work well enough for Moroccan women, she could not believe that she would be afforded the same protection. "I have had a long day, and I am weary. I think I would prefer to stay where I am." Her refusal would be a good test of how far the protection of the women's quarters extended to her.

Layla nodded approvingly and spoke a few sharp words to the servant, who ran back the way she had come.

Louisa listened apprehensively for any sign that her refusal had been received with anger, but there was nothing—not even an attempt to persuade her, to change her mind. Layla had spoken the truth. Here in the women's quarters she was safe. Slowly but surely she began to relax, and to enjoy the company of the women around her.

As the night began to fall and the temperature dropped, brass lanterns were lit around the edge of the terrace, bathing the rooftop in a golden glow. Louisa wrapped her shawl snugly around her shoulders, though she hardly needed it for the warmth. Even in Italy she could not have sat outside with such comfort as night fell.

After dark, dinner was served, still on the rooftop terrace. The women of the household gathered around a circular table, sitting on cushions without a thought of the damage the dew might cause to the fabric.

Louisa took her place among them, and a round dish of meat was placed in the middle of the table. A basin of water was offered to each person at the table, and a trickle of fresh water was poured over their hands to wash. Then Layla murmured a few words under her breath, and gestured at them all to start eating.

No cutlery was provided. They ate, Louisa noticed, only with their right hands, taking the food from that part of the bowl closest to them, never reaching past their neighbor for a choicer morsel. Clumsily, she followed suit, picking morsels of food out of the communal bowl, dipping the flat bread in gravy, and eating it all with her fingers.

This was how Khair Bey had shown her to eat when they were back in Italy. A wave of longing for him swept over her, so strong that it caught in her breast. If she had not refused his invitation to dine with him, just to see if she could, right now she would be sharing an intimate meal with him. He would be picking choice tidbits out of the bowl for her, and feeding them to her with his own hands . . .

It was just as well she had refused the invitation. She knew only too well how such a meal like that would end. She knew the limits of her own strength. Whatever her original intentions, such a dinner would inevitably lead her straight to

Khair Bey's bed. She was not ready for that. She might never be ready.

But Layla had offered her a choice—a real choice. She looked around the table at the women sharing the meal with her and smiled. She felt safe here, as she never had felt before.

Khair Bey was drinking coffee in the courtyard the following morning when his mother whirled in with the force of a desert sandstorm. Deprived of Louisa's company, he had slept badly and his usually sharp mind felt heavy and fogged over. He greeted her with a grim mockery of a smile, unable to summon more, even for his mother.

"You have not been honest with your intended bride." His mother's voice was sharp with displeasure as she flounced to a stop in front of him. "You have lied to her."

He knew very well that his mother was behind Louisa's refusal to dine with him the previous night. Left to herself, Louisa would have succumbed to the politely worded request. His mother had not only allowed but also abetted Louisa's rebellion against his wishes. "What have I said to her that is untrue?"

If his mother was angry with him, he was equally angry with her. She had been the cause of his ruined evening and the emptiness of his bed. Louisa would never acclimatize herself to living here with him if she was protected on all sides by his traitorous female relatives. No, he would sooner turn them all out of his house to find shelter with their other—less wealthy, less generous—family members than brook their continued interference in his life.

"Pirates, pah!" She positively spat the words out. "Since when have pirates plagued the Barbary Coast, taking slaves to sell in the marketplace? Not since I was a girl, I can tell you. And these so-called pirates accidentally happened on the ship that coincidentally carried the young Englishwoman you met in Italy—the woman you want to marry, but who clearly does not care a fig for you?

"And then they captured her and took her to a brothel to sell her there to the highest bidder, who just happened to be you?" She snapped her fingers with derision. "You will forgive me if I cannot believe a word of this ridiculous story."

Though he had known his mother would see through his story, he had not expected her to be so angry about it. After all, she had been captured and brought to his father's harem in much the same way, and she had always seemed content with her lot as the pampered favorite of a wealthy bey. "I have not asked you to."

"You have asked Louisa to believe it. She thinks that you have bought her as your concubine, as your love slave—as if I would allow such goings-on in my riad."

He forbore mentioning that the riad belonged to him, and not to her. In the temper she was in, there was no point antagonizing her further.

His mother was not appeased by his silence. She stormed up and down in front of him, her hands clenched into fists at her sides. "You wanted her but she would not have you, so you stole her."

He shrugged. What was done was done. He would not be ashamed of his actions. They had been necessary to secure his will. "She is here now. That is all that matters."

To his surprise, his mother stepped forward and slapped him on the side of his head, hard enough to make him see stars. Her cheeks were bright red patches of fury on her usually composed face, and her eyes were burning with what looked almost like hatred.

He blinked at her, confused. In all his life, she had never raised a hand to him before. She had never struck anyone, not even the laziest and most disobedient of her servants. The shock of it temporarily robbed him of the power of speech.

"I brought you up better than to steal a woman away from her family, from her home, from everything she holds dear," she spat at him. "You have brought *hshuma* to your name and to the name of your family by your actions. You shame me. You shame yourself."

"She is my woman," he said doggedly. The hatred in his mother's eyes unnerved him, though he did not show it. His mother had cared for him and loved him all his life. "She gave herself to me of her own free will. All I have done is bind her to me more tightly."

"That is no excuse. She is an Englishwoman, not a Berber. She knows nothing of such bargains."

"In time she will accept her fate."

"As I have done?" His mother laughed bitterly. The sound echoed through the air, bouncing back on him from the hills on either side of the valley until it seemed as though he would drown in it. "I never forgave your father for what he did to me. Never. He brought me here without a thought for what I wished, and then I discovered that I was nothing more than a passing fancy to him, another pretty bauble to add to his collection. He robbed me of a normal life, the sort of life I had been brought up to lead, the only life I wanted. I would have been happier as the wife of a simple fisherman."

"I am not my father. I will make her happy." He would not shame Louisa by secretly filling his harem with local beauties and exotic dancing girls. His father had done this and claimed that they were all poor relatives of his, and he had a duty to bring them into his family and support them. It was just a coincidence that so many of his poverty-stricken relatives were handsome young women who were only too happy to visit his bed at night.

"Happiness is not a gift you can bestow on another. Let her go, son."

His mother asked too much of him. "I cannot do that. She belongs to me."

"Let her go, or she will learn to hate, as I have done."

"I will take the risk, for you have also learned to love."

She turned her back on him then, and walked away. "Then you will do a foolish thing," she said over her shoulder. "And you must pay the price."

★ ★ ★

The hours stretched into days, and the days stretched into weeks as Louisa adjusted to life in the riad.

In the mornings, Khair Bey courted her—there was no other word for it. Shortly after the sun rose, he would take her out on excursions—a ride around the countryside on the pretty bay mare, with him on his stallion at her side; an amble around the streets of the casbah on the back of a friendly, gentle-eyed donkey as he led her by the reins; even once he took her out on the swaying back of a camel, which kneeled in front of her so she could climb onto it. She wasn't so fond of the camel—it drew its lips back over its teeth in a snarl, and spat.

They strolled among the almond groves; and visited the souk, where he bought her a brightly colored scarf and a necklace made of beads of silver and carved amber. Once, when it had rained overnight and the paths were muddy, they stayed in the riad and he strummed on the *guembri*—a lute with three strings—and sang to her lilting melodies that told of love and longing.

And he talked to her. He talked of his love for his homeland, and of the mountainous Rif and the land stretching to the sea. He discussed with her the difficulties he had being the bey—dispensing justice fairly to all his people, and to be seen as evenhanded, not favoring one over another. He asked for her opinions, and listened to her gravely when she gave them. But most of all, he spoke of how he longed to be alone with her, and of all the pleasure he would give her when it was just the two of them together, with no one else around.

But they were never quite alone. There could be no repeat of the liberties he had taken with her in the cypress grove in the Winterbottoms' garden in Italy. The casbah was always crowded with people going about their business. The fields outside the village walls were intensively cultivated, and wherever they went there were men and women working not far away. At the river, there would be children playing and splashing in the shallows, or a string of donkeys brought down to drink. Nowhere was there enough privacy for Khair Bey to do more than ride alongside her, or to maybe take her hand in his for a few moments as they walked.

Even when they stayed indoors, servants came and went through the house, carrying out their duties as they needed to, and the sounds of the *guembri* brought others who came to sit cross-legged on the floor and listen.

They would eat the midday meal together in the courtyard, sitting side by side and sharing food from the same bowl. Then, when their eating was done, he would bid her farewell and go about his business as the leader of his people.

During the sleepy afternoon hours, while Khair Bey was riding around the fields to supervise the workers, poring over the accounts, or dispensing justice, Louisa sat with the women of the household, learning how to make the intricately embroidered belts and slippers worn by the Berber men, or watching them at their looms, weaving finely patterned carpets. She could hardly believe how quickly their fingers skimmed over the loom, almost too fast for her to follow.

In the late afternoon, when the sun's heat had lost its fierceness, she and Layla might walk out together, with one of the male servants to accompany them, to the small local souk to purchase exotic spices for the household, or visit one of Layla's friends to sit in the shade, drink mint tea, and eat slices of orange sprinkled with cinnamon or almond-flavored pastries.

Every evening when the sun went down, the same request came from Khair Bey to dine with him, and every evening she refused in favor of dining in the women's quarters. The women did not make her feel like an outsider, but instead treated her as a treasured member of their family. They genuinely liked her, and she was growing very fond of them in return.

Taking a midday meal with Khair Bey in the courtyard was one thing, but dining with him alone in his room was quite another. Accepting his offer was tantamount to accepting her role as his mistress—his *captive* mistress, there only to please him, with no will of her own.

Though she spent each morning in anticipation, waiting in a fever of desire for those brief touches of his hand on hers, an accidental brush of his body, or the innocent touch of their legs when their horses passed too close to each other, she could not give in to him. She dared not give in.

What would happen to her mornings, the favorite part of her day, if Khair Bey no longer felt the need to court her so assiduously? Would he leave her with the women all day, bringing her to his rooms every night just to lie with her? Would her worth be devalued in his eyes, until she was nothing more to him than a convenient vessel for him to spill his seed into? If she gave in to him, would he lose interest in her once she no longer posed a challenge?

She loved the mornings spent in his company. She could see in his eyes how much he desired her, and read in his body language his frustration at not being able to touch her. Though his loose cotton trousers usually concealed his state of desire, the merest accidental touch made his back stiffen as if he was in pain, or elicited a groan as if he were being tortured by all the devils in hell. Giving in to his seduction would take the edge off his appetite for her, and leave him feeling comfortably sated instead of hungry.

By keeping him at a distance, she kept his attention—and more important, she kept her self-respect. As long as she could resist him, she knew that she was still Louisa Clemens, not just Khair Bey's woman. As long as she did not succumb to temptation, she had a measure of self-determination, if not of freedom.

He was not the only one who was suffering; their closeness was a torment to her, just as it was to him. Her whole body hummed with awareness in his presence. Despite the warmth of the early mornings, her nipples were permanently peaked as though with cold. They thrust toward him, wanting to feel his hands on them, his mouth teasing them, his tongue licking them.

The merest touch of his hand on hers was enough to make her body flood with heat and a damp patch to start growing between her legs. Her pussy burned with such desire; she longed to slake her need by rubbing herself against him while they talked.

She wanted to take his cock in her hands and watch it swell and grow hard as she bent down to take the head into her mouth. She wanted to lift her skirts and beg him to stroke her, to enter her, to thrust inside her until she screamed with fulfilment. She wanted him lying on his back, with his cock thrusting up into the air, and she wanted to ride it as she rode her mare in the mornings—slowly at first, and then faster and harder until she collapsed on top of him, breathless and sweating from the exertion.

But she did none of those things. She learned how to ride. She discovered the paths of the casbah and the enticing goods on display at the souk. She learned how durum wheat was harvested, when to gather almonds, and where the best olive trees grew. She learned to appreciate the stark beauty of the country, and to love the sound of running water, which promised a respite from the heat.

And she learned that Khair Bey was a man of fierce pride and even fiercer loyalties—a man whose love was not won easily, but once won, was won forever.

In her more optimistic moments, she even began to suspect that she had captured his heart.

One evening, the women were fizzing with an unaccustomed excitement that continued throughout the dinner hour. Though by now she had learned a few words of Berber, she did not understand a single thing they were trying to explain to her. She finally turned to Layla; even she, usually so calm and collected, was more animated than usual. "What is all the fuss about?"

"There is an exhibition tomorrow. A *harrqa*. With horses."

Louisa shrugged. An exhibition of horses did not seem enough to get so excited about. There were horses everywhere in Morocco, from the stocky barbs used as saddle horses to the purebred Arabians, whose owners prized them for their grace and beauty as much as for their endurance under the fierce Moroccan sun.

Layla must have read the confusion on her face. "You must forgive us. We Moroccans love our horses, and the men who ride them. When tomorrow comes, you will understand why."

The next morning, all the women were up early and dressed in their best. When Khair Bey came to the women's quarters, they broke into such a twittering of excitement that Louisa could hardly hear herself think above the din.

She had to admit feeling somewhat excited herself. Instead of his usual clothes, Khair Bey was dressed all in white: a long-sleeved white tunic, white baggy trousers, and even a white cap on his head instead of his usual red fez. Adding the only bit of color were his knee-high boots of bright yellow leather, covered in intricate embroidery. She had never seen him look quite so grand before.

"You have a special treat in store for you today," he explained, as he led her down to the courtyard, followed by the rest of the women of the harem. "Today I am riding in a *harrqa*."

"What is a *harrqa*? Your mother said something about it being an exhibition of horses."

Her words made him laugh. "That is like calling the ocean a puddle or the mighty mountains of the Rif a rise in the ground. But I cannot describe it. You will soon see for yourself."

He led the way to a recently cleared wheat field at the edge of the casbah, where a large group of people had already gathered. In one corner was a stand of horses, with bright red, tasseled harnesses around their necks. On their backs were blankets of embroidered silk, and perched on top of the blankets were high-backed saddles covered in ornate cloth. As she drew closer, she noticed that their eyes were covered with embroidered blinkers to severely restrict their vision.

Khair Bey took the reins of the largest horse, a jet-black stallion even more ornately decorated than the rest. "I must leave you here," he said, as he vaulted into the saddle and grabbed a long rifle held out to him by one of the men on the ground. "Enjoy the spectacle."

Layla stepped up and took Louisa's arm as they watched Khair Bey and the rest of the men on horseback wheel their horses around and ride to one end of the wheat field. Then, with a shout, the first riders were off. Khair Bey was in front, practically standing upright in his stirrups as he galloped full tilt down the field. The horses' hooves pounded on the dry ground, sending clouds of dust swirling into the air. Another shout and all the men lifted their rifles into the air and shot in unison. The boom reverberated around the valley like a tremendous thunderclap, sending clouds of birds squawking in the air for miles around.

Wave after wave of men on their horses galloped down the wheat field, firing their guns simultaneously into the air as they rode, until it looked as if there were a sea of horses and men rolling inexorably over the land. As each wave came to the end of the course, they wheeled around to the sides and cantered back to the start, ready to begin the wild gallop all over again.

The wheat field was churned into a mass of dust like foam on a wave, until they could hardly see the horses through the veil of obscurity that clouded them.

Beside her, the women were making almost as much noise as the horses, screaming their delight at a particularly wild gallop or their appreciation for a fine rider, or yelling insults when a rider mistimed his rifle shot. Their screams of delight turned to howls of terror when one of the riders lost his seating and teetered precariously, almost falling underneath the thundering hooves, before being pulled back up into his saddle by the man riding alongside him.

Caught up in the excitement, Louisa peered through the thickening clouds of dust, watching Khair Bey as he galloped and wheeled across the field in a stunning display of horsemanship, firing his rifle into the air as he rode at top speed. Not once did he falter or mistime his shot. It was as if man and beast were one, so beautifully did they work together.

Her eyes were smarting with grit and her ears ringing with the noise of the rifles being fired when the waves of horses and men finally slowed and then came to a stop.

The spectators came streaming onto the field, milling around the horses with excited chatter.

Louisa stayed where she was, watching as Khair Bey, still on horseback, made his way toward her.

She could not help drinking in the sight of him. In his ceremonial clothes, their whiteness now covered in dust and streaked with gunpowder residue from his rifle, he looked handsomer than ever. How wonderful he had been out there in the field, galloping at the head of his riders like a general at the head of a conquering army. How proud she had been to watch him. She longed to reach out and take him in her arms, to whisper in his ear how much she had missed him, how much she longed to kiss him, to touch him, to be his woman in every way he wanted her to be.

He vaulted easily off the back of his stallion and threw the reins to a waiting groom. "*That* is a *harrqa*," he said, drawing her into a brief embrace.

Louisa laughed at the sheer joy of being in his arms. He

smelled of sweat and horse and dirt, and she wished she could stay holding him forever. "It was not an exhibition—it was a thunderstorm. I thought I was going to be swallowed up in it."

He smiled happily as he took her arm and led her away from the horses and the crowds to a quieter part of the grounds. "I *was* swallowed up in it," he said. "When you are riding, you can think of nothing but the horse beneath you, and the rifle in your hand. Nothing else exists."

They had left the people and the noise behind them now, and were skirting a field of ripened wheat that had not yet been reaped. He took hold of her hand and pulled her in among the sheaves. The stalks towered up to their shoulders as they pushed their way in.

Laughing, he sank to his knees, and pulled her with him. The noise of the crowd was nothing but a distant murmur. "This is the first time I have been alone with you since you came to my home. Truly alone."

The sheaves of wheat hid them from view. All she could see was the blue sky above them. She nestled into his embrace. "We have spent every morning together," she protested, though she knew that was not what he meant.

He lay back in the wheat and gazed at her. "I confess I was hoping for something rather different when I paid such an outrageous sum of money to rescue you from the brothel. It's just as well for my reputation as a businessman that I do not make a habit of allowing myself to be gulled."

"I promised you nothing."

"True." He reached out and twined a lock of her hair around one finger, tugging her gently closer to him. "But listening to the old lady describe your many and manifold virtues, I thought I would be buying myself a most compliant and experienced mistress. Instead I got a prickly young miss who persists in refusing me."

Experienced? The only experience she had ever received had been at his hands. "Nonsense," she said, slapping his hand away, "you thought nothing of the kind. You knew me better than that. Besides, it is your own fault if you are dissatisfied. You gave me a choice whether or not to come to you at night. I chose to decline." Looking at him lying at his ease in front of her, she had to question the wisdom of her decision. Surely she had punished him, and herself, enough. He had saved her from the slave markets, after all, and bought her only to rescue her from falling into worse hands.

Though technically she belonged to him, he had never taken advantage of his ownership. She was free to become his lover, or to turn him down as she pleased. She had tested her power of refusal to the limit, and it had held firm. Though he might tease her about belonging to him, he treated her with nothing but respect.

The only thing she could not do was leave him, to return to her family in England.

A dreadful thought crossed her mind as she lay in the grass. What if he had found another woman to tend to him while she was sulking in the women's quarters? He was a man, not a eunuch, and he had a man's needs. She could not expect him to wait for her forever. The thought of him touching another woman in desire made her stomach clench in knots. She was the woman he desired—no one else.

Even if he were to set her free, to offer to return her to England, would she accept? She had grown to love Morocco, and to love him, more with each day that passed. Leaving him would be like leaving a part of herself.

His eyes became dark with something that looked like anger and he rolled away from her. "Are you suggesting I order you to do as I wish? Or force myself on you?"

A shiver of revulsion chilled her spine. "No, never that." If he ever tried to force her, she would truly learn to hate him.

"Then come to me now, Louisa. Come and kiss me."

"Is that an order?" As much as she wanted him, an order would be easy to refuse. She did not care how much money had passed hands when he rescued her—she was not his slave. She would never be his slave.

Once again he reached toward her, this time brushing her cheek with the back of his hand. "It has never been an order, only an invitation. A very sincere, deeply felt invitation that has been getting more sincere and deeply felt every day."

An invitation was so much harder to refuse than an order —especially when it was accompanied by a pleading look in those proud gray eyes of his, eyes that were so much more used to commanding obedience than begging for favors. Her heart ached to make them smoulder with desire, with love for her.

He sensed her softening toward him and took the opportunity to bring her down beside him. His lips were on hers and he was kissing her, tenderly at first and then with a growing passion.

She had wanted him for so long that his kiss was like a spark on a pile of tinder, setting off an instant conflagration that was beyond her power to control. All she could do was let it burn higher and hotter, until it temporarily burned itself out.

As their kiss deepened, she slipped her hand inside his shirt, needing to feel the beat of his heart, to know that it was beating for her.

He groaned as her hands slid over his naked skin, and the fire took him as well. Pushing up her skirts, he slipped his hand between her legs, reaching unerringly for that part of her that cried out for him.

She was already wet for him. She could feel the moisture on his fingers as he stroked her, dipping his fingers into her and then stroking her between the thighs, building up the tension in her until she wanted to scream at him to give her the release she craved. Nothing else mattered but the ache between her thighs and the desperate need she had to be filled.

His cock was thrust up hard against her opened thigh, insistent in its pressure. He moved her hand down to touch him. "Please, Louisa. Touch me as I am touching you."

Yes, she wanted his cock in her hands, just as her pussy was in his. Working with feverish haste, she undid the buttons on his trousers and freed his proud cock. A couple of strokes, and the veins were standing out on his member, and a few drops of come started to seep out of the tip. As she swirled the milky fluid around the head of his cock, he pulled away from her. "I've wanted you too long to come in your hand like a green schoolboy," he panted. "I need to fuck you, Louisa. I need to thrust my cock deep into your pussy, and come inside you."

With a groan, he pushed his trousers down over his hips and moved on top of her. His cock slid over the entrance to her pussy, coating itself in her juices. "Please, Louisa. Take me inside you."

She was as desperate for him as he was for her. In answer, she pulled her skirts out of the way, bunching them up at her waist. With her hands on his buttocks, she guided him into her, until he was buried deep inside her.

It felt as though she were flying, as if she had been set free from everything that bound her to the earth. Though in her mind she knew she was lying on bare ground, on trampled stalks of ripened wheat, her body could feel only the fierce joy of possessing and of being possessed.

This was no time for finesse or careful loving. Their mutual need made such things unnecessary, undesirable. There was only a frantic haste driven by desperation and by the fear that they would be discovered. Powerfully, he thrust into her, each time filling her with a sense of completion and taking her nearer to the brink.

It was only a few thrusts before he held himself over her, his face contorted with the effort of control. "I have waited too long for this," he groaned, his teeth gritted with the effort. "I cannot hold on any longer."

She was so close to an orgasm herself that having him stop would be torture. "You do not need to," she said, bucking herself against him, driving him deeper into her. "Let it go. Bring me with you."

By permitting him to lose himself in her, and admitting that she was as close to climax as he was, Louisa finally drove him over the edge. With one last thrust, he shuddered inside her, his seed infusing her with a rush of warmth. As she felt his essence flooding into her, her own orgasm hit her with a wave of pleasure that went on as if it would never stop. Her back arched off the ground and, despite the possibility of discovery, she was unable to stop herself from crying out.

On and on, the convulsions continued, as he wrung every last drop of pleasure out of both of them. Only then did he withdraw and collapse beside her, utterly spent.

He smoothed her skirts back over her legs and held her close to him as if he never wanted to let her go. "Come to me tonight, Louisa. Let me love you as you are meant to be loved—slowly and reverently, in silk sheets and luxury, with care and love. Not this hurried coupling of animals in the fields. You were not made for this."

Louisa sighed with satisfaction in his arms, uncaring of the prickles of wheat grass on her back and legs. Why did something as beautiful as they had shared have to be labeled a sin? There should be nothing sinful in giving another person pleasure, and finding pleasure for yourself at the same time. Men and women were made for each other, whether it was in fields of wheat or on sheets of satin.

Did it truly matter if she was to repeat her sin and take him as her lover? She was living in Morocco now, where the way of life was so different from how people lived in England. His household would not condemn her for her weakness; they had already accepted her as one of their own, and no one in England need ever know of her shame.

And she wanted him. Oh, how she wanted him. Even now, lying sated in his arms, she wanted nothing else. "If you wish me to," she whispered, "I will come to you tonight."

"For weeks I have wished for nothing else."

"Then send for me tonight, and I will come."

The smile that lit his eyes was worth the misgiving she felt in her heart. After so many weeks of craving his touch, she knew she would not be able to resist the temptation that he offered her. Their recent desperate coupling had proven that much.

Meeting him alone could have only one outcome. In her heart, she had already given in to his seduction and was lying naked and panting in front of him, her thighs spread wide apart, her pussy gaping wetly open, begging for him to come and take her.

This morning had not been planned—they had come together out of need and desperation. It had been an aberration, an opportunity seen and seized.

Dining with him tonight, however, would be an act of deliberation, a definite decision. She would not be able to hide behind the excuse of being overcome by the force of circumstance, of being overwhelmed by the sudden strength of her need.

As soon as they were alone together, the moment she deliberately put herself under his power, she would become the eager and compliant mistress he wanted her to be.

Eight

That afternoon, Louisa spent longer than usual in the hammam, scrubbing herself all over first with hot water and then with cold, having almond-scented oil rubbed into her skin, and brushing her hair until it shone. If Khair Bey wanted to shower her with luxury as he had promised, she would prove herself worthy of it. She would show him that she was destined for better things than to be casually tumbled in the wheat fields.

When the knock on the door came, as it always did in the evenings, she was almost trembling with anticipation. This evening she would become Khair Bey's mistress in her heart and her soul, as she already was in her body.

Layla poured another cup of mint tea for Louisa, expecting her refusal. "My son is persistent," she murmured, almost as if in apology, as she poured. "But I think he has met his match in you."

There was no apology needed—not tonight. Louisa nodded gracefully at the servant bearing the message. "I will be glad to dine with Khair Bey," she said, as she pushed aside her tea and rose from the divan. "Please thank him for the invitation and tell him I will be with him in a moment."

Layla raised her eyebrows at Louisa's sudden change of heart. "There is no need for you to go. You know that." Her face looked troubled, as if she were chewing over a thought in her mind. "You can stay here if you would rather, and he will not bother you. I will see to that."

"I know that I can stay here, and I thank you for the knowledge." She gave Layla a grateful glance. "But that is why tonight I will go—because I know I do not have to."

Layla pursed her lips together. "You wish to make your own choice in the matter?"

"I do."

The older woman nodded then, almost as if she were giving Louisa her blessing. "Go, then."

Khair Bey was waiting at the door to the women's quarters, tension written all over his body. As soon as he saw her, it flowed out of him and a sigh of relief escaped his lips. He took her hand and carried it to his lips. "You took so long, I was concerned you might have thought better of your promise."

His nervousness endeared him to her all the more. He had not taken her consent for granted, or arrogantly assumed because she had come to him once, that she would come to him again. "I gave you my word that I would come."

"You could still have changed your mind," he said, as he led her through the house to his own private quarters. "I half expected you would think better of your promise after I attacked you in the wheat field today with all the finesse of a ravening lion." Though the hallway was dark, she was sure she could see a flush stain his cheeks with red.

"You would not have been angry with me?"

"Angry? No. But I would have been very disappointed. I have been looking forward to spending an evening in your company. Just the two of us. We have not been together like this since Italy." He pushed open the door to his apartment and ushered her in. "I never thought I would feel nostalgic for anyplace other than my own home, but I will make an exception for that night in Italy when I fed you figs and almonds and loved you for the first time."

Her room in the women's quarters was beautiful, opulent even, compared to what she was used to, but it could not hold a candle to Khair Bey's apartment. The floor was tiled in an intricate mosaic pattern, as was her own, but while her walls were made of plain plaster, here the mosaic tiling continued halfway up the wall in swirls of glorious color. The higher half of the walls and the ceiling were made of plaster carved into shapes that reminded her of honey hives. Set into the walls were windows of stained glass that sent a rainbow of colors through the room.

The carpets on the floor were fine and soft, and the low divan in one corner was upholstered in silk and covered with mounds of silk cushions.

She looked around in awe. It felt as though she had stepped into the pages of a fairy tale, a story from *One Thousand and One Nights*. She almost expected a bevy of dancing girls with bells around their wrists and ankles to writhe sinuously in, dancing to the music of their tambourines, or a genie to appear in a puff of smoke from a lantern. It was a room fit for a king, a sultan—for a prince of princes.

He laughed at the expression on her face. "You like my room?"

"It is so beautiful I can't bear to touch anything in case I spoil it."

He took her in his arms and twirled her around the room until she was dizzy. "My room is made for loving and for being loved. All that was missing was you."

"I am here tonight."

"My beautiful Louisa. Before this morning, I was beginning to wonder if I would ever be able to tempt you back into my arms."

She felt a tide of color creep into her cheeks at the reminder of her wanton behavior in the wheat field. All he needed was to get her alone, and she was lost to all sense of herself. Time and again he had proven her weakness for him. "I know I should not be here . . ."

"Do not say that!" He took her face in his hands and looked deeply into her eyes, as if he could convince her with the sheer force of his will. "Never say that you do not belong with me."

She did not know anymore where she truly belonged. "I belong with you tonight," she temporized. That was enough for her at the moment.

"Indeed you do." It seemed to be enough for him, too. Tomorrow would bring its own challenges, but tonight was for them to share. "Are you hungry?"

She eyed the plates of food piled on a table in the corner, from which an appetizing smell arose. Moroccan cuisine was delicious. Ordinarily she would love to sample all the dishes and taste every exotic flavor, but not tonight. Eating could wait. She ran her hands over his chest, toying with his buttons. "Not for food. For you."

"Then let me sate your appetite. Let me love you as you deserve to be loved."

"Take me to bed," she whispered to him, quietly surrendering herself. "Make me your woman."

Kneeling at her feet, he removed her embroidered slippers, first one and then the other, before reaching up to loosen her garters and unroll her stockings. When her fingers moved to her bodice to unbutton her shirt, he stopped her by placing his own hand over hers. "Please, let me. I want to undress all of you. I want to worship every inch of you as I go."

At his behest she stood still, allowing him to undress her as he pleased. After he had removed her stockings, he untied her skirts, letting them puddle at her feet. Her bodice was next. With great care, he undid every tiny button, and then pushed the fabric over her shoulders. "You have such beautiful skin," he murmured, smoothing his hands over her arms and neck.

She stepped out of her skirts, standing in front of him dressed only in a light linen shift and drawers. The days in Morocco were too warm to wear the layers of petticoats and the tightly boned corsets she had been used to wearing in England, and even in Italy.

"You look like every man's wicked fantasy," he murmured, as he sat back on a pile of cushions on the floor and just looked up at her. "Turn around, so I can admire all of you."

Obediently, she gave a little pirouette, waggling her hips just a little as she moved.

"Take off the rest of your clothes," he ordered from his position on the floor. "I want to see you naked."

"I thought you were going to undress me," she pouted.

"I have changed my mind. I want to watch you as you undress yourself."

His desire for her was etched deeply in his expression. She wanted to make him mad for her, as she had been for him earlier that morning. She wanted him to be prepared to give up the world to have her.

She pushed the straps of her shift off her shoulders and slowly pushed it down her body. Her breasts bobbed free, her nipples already hard. Taking them in her hands, she leaned forward, offering them to him. They were all his, as all of her belonged to him tonight.

He crooked a finger at her. "Come over here."

"Not yet." There were still her drawers to go. Not until she was totally naked, without any artifice to hide herself, would she go to him.

The drawstrings that held her drawers together were knotted, but a short, sharp tug freed them. She held them there for a moment, and then allowed them to drop. Bare as the day she was born, she stood in front of him.

When he beckoned to her this time, she went willingly to him, dropping down on the cushions to join him. Her breasts were aching for his touch. He must have heard their silent plea, for he took them into his hands as he kissed her, kneading them until her nipples were like tiny pebbles. Every caress sent shivers of heat through her body, until all her nerves were on fire. Though she had been in his company for only a few minutes, she was already wet and ready for him. He could fuck her fast and hard right now, and she would be with him all the way, just as she had been in the field that morning.

But she knew he wasn't going to take her quickly tonight. This would be no rushed and hurried coupling, as when they'd desperately slaked each other's needs so that they would not be discovered tumbling in the grass. He would prolong the pleasure, drawing out their lovemaking until she was senseless with need.

"Lie there," he instructed her, as he stood up in his turn. "Now you may watch me."

She could only lie back on the cushions as he undressed for her, just as she had for him. First his embroidered slippers, and then his *djelleba*, the hooded robe he wore. He pushed his trousers and his drawers over his lean hips in one fluid movement, and whipped his shirt over his head.

His skin was a rich brown, tanned to a deep chocolate on his forearms. Even his cock, standing up stiff and proud, was brown, though the head was a dark pink. His thighs were hard and muscular, and his buttocks taut and firm. Even his chest and stomach rippled with muscles.

She ran her hand over her own chest and down to her belly. Where she was soft, he was hard. Where he was firm, she was yielding.

Almost of its own volition, her hand crept lower to tangle in the curls of her pussy. That was where he was the hardest, and where she was the softest. She spread her thighs apart and dipped her finger between them to touch her folds. Her own touch sent a bolt of desire through her whole body. She wanted his hand on her there, she wanted that proud brown cock pushing into her, filling her up with its thick length.

She arched her back so he could see her better, and with deliberate provocation slipped one of her own fingers inside her pussy.

"That is my job," he growled at her, as he dropped to his knees between her legs. "I am the only one who should be putting my fingers in your pussy, the only one who should taste your sweetness, the only one to thrust my cock inside you and fill you with my come."

His words were making her hotter than ever. She wanted him to do all that to her—and more. Whatever he did to her tonight would make her scream with pleasure. She allowed him to pull her hand away, her finger dripping with her wetness. "Then taste me. Come inside me. Take me."

"You are too impatient," he said, as he moved his head between her thighs. "I need to make up for my haste this morning. Tonight I will savor every inch of you, not gulp you down as if I were starving."

True to his word, he started to taste her. She arched her back and screamed as he flicked over her sensitive folds with his tongue. The tickling sensation was almost too much for her to bear, and she writhed on the floor, not sure if she was trying to escape him or to beg for more.

He lifted his head for a moment, allowing her to catch her breath. "Do you want to taste me, too?"

She nodded, suddenly filled with a longing to have his cock in her mouth, to feel its ridges with her tongue, to lick all over the sensitive head.

He scooted around on the floor until he was lying over her, his face still buried in her pussy, but his cock now tantalizingly close to her mouth. She leaned up and licked the tip of it, where a tiny drop of come was seeping out. He tasted slightly salty, as if he had been swimming in the ocean.

At the flick of her tongue on him, he gave a groan and lowered himself down on top of her so she could reach him better. She needed no urging to take more of him into her mouth, and to suck on him until he groaned again.

His balls were hard and firm, almost completely retreated into his body. Wanting to know everything about him, she gave them an exploratory lick, just to see how sensitive they were, and was rewarded by the redoubling of his own attentions.

She was so intent on discovering every inch of him that she made a noise of protest when he finally pulled away from her.

"No more," he said, "or I shall come in your mouth before I even get to fuck you."

She wondered what it would be like to have him lose control and fill her mouth with his come. One of these days she would have to try it and see. But not today. Tonight she was as anxious as he was to have him inside her.

He got to his feet, took her in his arms and carried her into his bedroom. The bed was turned back, the silk sheets glowing in the light of the candles set around the room. Sprinkled on the sheets were dozens of rose petals, their heavy perfume filling the air. He laid her down gently on the bed. "This is where you belong," he murmured, "naked and covered in rose petals."

The petals tickled her. Squirming, she brushed them away and held out her arms to him. "And you belong beside me. On top of me. Inside me."

He joined her on the bed then, smoothing his hands over her skin as though he had never seen her before. She no longer wanted his gentleness—she wanted him to possess her, to make her his. She wanted him to fuck her hard and fast, to brand her with his ownership.

Squirming over onto her stomach, she got up on her hands and knees and thrust her backside into the air. It was a wordless plea for him to thrust inside her, and to her relief, it worked.

He knelt in between her legs, teasing her with the tip of his cock. Then, with one slow, sure thrust, he entered her, pushing all the way inside until he was buried to the hilt.

That was where he ought to be, where she needed him to be. She gently rocked forward and backward on her elbows, loving the feeling of him buried deep inside her.

He did not let her set the tempo for long. Slowly, inexorably, he pulled out of her, and then surged in once more. Time after time he entered her with a long, slow thrust, pausing each time he was deep inside her to let her luxuriate in the fullness of him, to let her truly feel that he completed her.

All too soon, the tremors in her body built up to a peak. Her orgasm was approaching, coming closer with every movement he made, unstoppable.

"Please," she begged him, pushing against him, urging him to enter her faster, deeper. She could not take much more of this torment before she would explode.

His pace quickened just a fraction, but it was enough to send her over the edge. A hard thrust, and she grabbed on to the head of the bed to steady herself as her body came apart in an explosion of sensation. She was flying, she was falling, she was dissolving into a thousand tiny fragments of herself. On and on it went, her pussy contracting and throbbing with delight, clutching him as if she never wanted to let him go.

Driven by his own need, he thrust into her blindly, until he joined her in mutual pleasure, his seed spilling out of him in a rush. He held there, poised over her, as they rode out their passion. Then, with a sigh of utter satisfaction, he collapsed onto the bed and took her into his arms, nuzzling his face into her neck with soft kisses. "That is how a woman should be loved. Not among the grass in the field."

Louisa allowed her eyes to drift shut as she luxuriated in the feeling of being in his arms. She had done it, she had become Khair Bey's mistress of her own free will, and she could not be sorry for it.

Some weeks later, Louisa sat by herself in the courtyard, watching the water in the fountain. The sound of it bubbling over the rim and falling into the pool below soothed her senses. The courtyard was her favorite part of the house, and this was her favorite part of the courtyard, the place where she came to be alone to sit and think. The other women preferred to gather on their rooftop terrace and sit in the cooling breeze, drinking mint tea and chattering, but as much as she had grown fond of them all, sometimes she loved to escape their company to sit by herself for a while.

Truthfully, her life in Morocco was not a bad one. Khair Bey continued to spend the mornings with her, but now he spent his nights with her as well. Though her afternoons were her own and she was free to sit with the other women, learning how to spin and weave beautiful cloth as they did, embroidering caftans—the long, loose robes they wore—or tending to the flowers in the courtyard garden, her evenings and her nights belonged to him.

Each evening he called for her to dine with him and she went to where he waited for her, in his room decorated like a sultan's palace. Each night she fought temptation and lost. He did not demand—rather he asked, and that was her undoing.

Knowing that she could refuse him made it all the harder to do so. He made her want him to the exclusion of everything else, even to the exclusion of her good sense. She was not ignorant of what would come of her giving in to his seduction. Sooner or later he would plant a babe in her belly, and then all hope of leaving here would be gone forever. Even if he freed her, she would have no choice but to remain his captive. England, and the English way of life, would be lost to her.

Her weakness was what troubled her the most. If only she could be strong and refuse to be Khair Bey's mistress, then at least she would have her self-respect to comfort her in her exile. But he could not even leave her with that. He robbed her of everything, leaving her nothing that she could cling to for hope. Sometimes she loved him so much, she almost hated him.

The rest of the time, she knew she did not hate him. What she felt for him was perilously close to love. She listened for his footsteps on the stairs, and the sound of his knock on the door that led to the women's quarters, asking for admission. When she was with him, she could think of nothing but the feel of his arms around her, the touch of his mouth on hers, the weight of his body as it pressed against her. He was like a drug to her, and she craved him as an addict craves laudanum, caring for nothing beyond the next taste.

And as soon as her craving was temporarily satisfied, she hated the need that she felt, hated her dependence on a man who would not allow her to be herself, and hated the way she was stuck here in limbo. She was not a wife, nor a servant. She had no duties or cares, and nothing useful to do but while away the daylight hours. She was a guest in a house that ought to be hers to command, but she was not able to command it. She hated it all until she saw him again, and was struck anew by her craving. Her fingers dabbled in the cold water of the fountain. Though she loved Morocco, this was no way to live.

"You are not happy here?" Unnoticed, Khair Bey's mother had come to sit beside her at the fountain.

"You have been everything that is kind and welcoming," Louisa replied. Even despite her embarrassing admissions on her arrival, Layla had always treated her with courtesy and kindness, and lent her a sympathetic ear when she had needed one.

"My son has not been so kind?"

"He, too, has been very kind. He does not treat me as his captive, but as a living, breathing human being. I am grateful to him for that."

"You have fallen in love with him, then? That is the cause of your unhappiness?"

Louisa shrugged, and to her horror, she felt her eyes fill with tears. "I don't know what to do."

Layla patted her on the shoulder. "Let me tell you a story." She fell silent then, for so long that Louisa raised her head, wondering if the older woman had forgotten what she was about to say. In her eyes was a faraway look as she began to speak. "There were pirates all over the Barbary Coast when I was a young girl. Slavers. They preyed on all the shipping that went through the Strait of Gibraltar, capturing the sailors and selling them in the marketplace of Tunis. It got so bad that merchants were afraid for their men and even more for their cargoes, so they sent men of war along with their fleets.

"But the pirates were bold and daring. When the ships fired back at them, they turned to easier prey. They sailed to Spain, to France, even to the coast of England. Unlike the big merchant fleets, small seaside towns were unprotected, and slaves were worth enough to make the journey worth their while.

"I was born in Brittany, in a fishing village right on the water. When I was a young girl, the slavers came, and I was taken and sold in the marketplace. A wealthy man bought me for his harem, and in time I became his favored concubine and bore him a son, Ithry."

"You are a Frenchwoman?" She had wondered why Layla was so much lighter-skinned than many of her countrywomen, and why her English, though spoken with a strong accent, was so good. Knowing that the older woman had been brought up in Brittany, just across the channel from England, explained much that had puzzled her.

"It has been a long while since I have thought of myself as anything but a Moroccan, but yes, I was once a Frenchwoman. I have not seen my home again since I was taken. Sometimes I even forget that I was born a Frenchwoman, that I once played barefoot on the beach in the sand and gathered shellfish for my dinner. Morocco, and the Moroccan way of life, is all I have known for so long."

"You never wanted to leave? To see your home and family again?"

Layla shrugged, her face bitter remembering her grief. "What are the wants and wishes of a favored concubine when set against her master's desires? Ithry's father was a hard man, and jealous of anything that belonged to him. He would never let me go." Her voice softened. "My son has done to you what his father did to me, despite my anger. I am sorry for it."

Louisa bowed her head. She wished she could argue, but she could not. Was it her fate to spend the rest of her life in a foreign country, never to see her family again, just as Khair Bey's mother had suffered before her?

"But Ithry has done worse than his father ever did." She laid a comforting hand on Louisa's arm. "He has deceived you. It was his men who took you from your ship, his men who took you to the brothel and pretended to sell you into slavery. And all of it because his pride could not bear to be refused by the woman he had his heart set on."

The words cut Louisa's heart into ribbons. "Pretended to sell me into slavery?" Was everything a sham? Had he made her suffer for nothing?

With sudden clarity, she recalled the moment on the pirate ship when she thought she had seen Khair Bey at the wheel— the moment that she thought was borne out of her desperate desire for rescue. It *had* been him after all. She had not imagined seeing him. He had terrified her half out of her wits and put her through the worst kind of torment, all for the sake of his pride?

"Maybe he thought you would be grateful to him for rescuing you from slavers. Maybe he thought you would be more obedient to his dictates if you thought you were a slave. He captured you, that is true, but does that make you subject to his whim?" She shook her head vehemently. "No man, not even my son, has the right to take a woman's freedom, not even if the law allows it."

"Then I am free to leave here? To go home?" The longing to see England again, to be among her own family—people who loved her and would not betray her—was suddenly so great that it made her double over in pain.

"Free?" The older woman gave an ugly laugh. "When is a woman ever free to do as she pleases?"

"I have to remain here?" Her disappointment was bitter on her tongue.

"My son wishes to marry you. You have seen the lengths he has already gone to in order to get you here. He will not let you go easily."

"He wants to marry me? But he has never said anything to me. Not since Italy." She shook her head. The sun suddenly seemed blinding, and the heat in the courtyard stifling. "I thought he had put aside that notion now that I am his regardless of whether he weds me or not. Are you quite sure he specifically mentioned marriage?"

"He introduced you to me on the first day he brought you here as the woman he was going to marry. He would never have brought you here otherwise—not to live in the same household as his own mother, and in the home he loves best."

Louisa felt sick to her stomach. "I cannot marry him. He does not deserve me."

"No, he does not." Layla looked as if she, too, was near tears.

"He has taken away my freedom, deceived me, used me, and made me hate myself for loving him."

"So you do love him, then?"

"When I do not hate him."

The older woman heaved a sigh. "I knew how it would be, but he would not listen to my warning. You must leave here, Louisa, both for his sake and for your own."

"I would if I could, but where would I go? How would I get there? I know so little of the country, and nothing of the language. And I have no money, nothing even to barter for my passage home."

Layla took one of Louisa's hands in her own. "Let me take care of that. I hoped my son would be honest with you. I hoped you would come to love him as he loves you, but it is not to be. You are not happy here. I have waited longer than I should have. My son has done you a great wrong, and I will right it if I can."

"He will be very angry if you help me."

"That is my problem, do not worry yourself. Tomorrow morning, early, I will have a man waiting for you by the stables. He is a good man and will take you to the coast and pay for your passage back to England."

She would never forget the older woman's kindness. "Thank you. How can I ever repay you?"

A sad smile lightened her features. "Think of my son kindly

when you are gone. His pride has driven him to behave like this. Truly, he is not a bad man, just a foolish one, as all men are foolish sometimes."

The first gray of dawn was just lightening the sky when Louisa sneaked out of the house and made her way over the bare ground to the stables. She stopped for a moment while her eyes adjusted to the deeper darkness inside the barn. It was all quiet, with only a faint rustling and the noise of the horses' breathing to break the silence.

There was no sign yet of the servant who Layla had promised would come to assist her, but she was reluctant to wait for him. Delaying her departure meant that she ran the risk of being discovered. Now that she knew the full extent of Khair Bey's deception, she would attempt the journey alone rather than remain in servitude. Layla had given her enough money to hire a guide to the coast and pay for a boat to carry her to England.

Stepping softly, she made her way down the row of stalls. In the stall closest to the door she could make out the silhouette of Khair Bey's black stallion. She thought for a moment about letting him out into the courtyard to slow any pursuit that might follow her, but she could not bring herself to do it. He was a beautiful horse, and she would never forgive herself if he was damaged on her account.

A few stalls farther down, she found what she was looking for—the sweet-tempered chestnut mare Khair Bey had taught her to ride on. The mare was not the fastest horse in the stable, but she was easily managed, and Louisa was not a very confident horsewoman. After slipping a bridle over Zahra's head, she unbolted the stall and led the animal out.

A saddle would make her riding easier, but she did not have the time to heft up a saddle and fasten the girth tight enough that she could be sure of not falling off. Instead, she grabbed a couple of thick woolen blankets and threw them over the mare's back. Though they would not stay on if she were to kick the mare into a fast trot, they would cushion her bottom as well as a saddle. She was not comfortable enough on horseback that she was planning to trot much anyway. Surprise, not speed, would be her ticket to freedom. If Khair Bey thought he had broken her spirit, he would soon find out she was made of stronger stuff than he ever suspected.

A shadow detached itself from the side of the stable. She suppressed a scream of fright. "Who are you?" she asked, her voice quivering. She hoped it was the man that Layla had promised to send, and not one of Khair Bey's spies. If Khair Bey had somehow found out her plan and sent someone to stop her, she would throw herself into the river rather than tamely submit.

"Layla send me," he explained to her in broken English.

She looked at the speaker and blinked. "You are one of the villagers? Khair Bey is your lord? And yet you would help me run away?"

He merely shook his head in reply. "Come."

The day was getting lighter by the second. She was not sure whether her guide was trustworthy, but if she was going to leave, she must do so now.

She could not stay. As much as she hated to run away from Khair Bey without telling him, she had no other choice. In Italy she had been honest with him about her reasons for leaving, and he had only pretended to let her go. His complaisance had been nothing but a sham. The only thing left for her to do was to run, and hope she could throw him off her scent for long enough to get away from him for good.

She pulled herself up onto the pile of blankets that served as her saddle and kicked the horse into motion. Her escort swung onto the back of a small donkey waiting patiently in the yard, and that Louisa had not noticed until now. Together, they rode out toward the hills that led to the coast.

Louisa did not look back at the walls of the village behind her as she rode away. Khair Bey lay sleeping, unaware of her departure, not knowing he had held her in his arms for the last time.

Tears ran down her cheeks as she rode away from him, away from the only man she had ever loved. She could not look back. She was afraid her heart would break.

Ithry Khair knocked eagerly on the door that led to the women's apartments. Last night, for the first time since they had reached a new accord, Louisa had declined his request to dine in his company and spend the night with him, citing women's troubles as her excuse, and then she had elected to stay indoors all this morning as well, instead of going walking with him.

Disappointed twice in a row, he had kept busy out in the olive groves seeing to his men since early morning, and he had missed her company. Surely she would not refuse him two nights in a row. He would not allow her to refuse him. Even if she were not in the mood for love, they could still dine together, and he could hold her in his arms as they slept. He would ask no more of her than that.

His mother came to answer his summons, waving him in to the spacious communal area. A smile broke over his face at the invitation to enter, which he had not received ever since he had brought Louisa to his home. Clearly his mother's resentment toward him was weakening. He was her only son, and he'd known she could not nurse her anger with him for very long.

He looked around eagerly for Louisa, but she was nowhere in sight. "Where is Louisa?"

His mother lifted her eyebrows. "Are you so impatient to be out of my company?"

He offered up a shamefaced smile. "My apologies, mother. I am eager to see her, that is all. She was not in the mood for my company last night, and I find that I miss her."

"Then I am very much afraid that you will not be pleased with the news I have to tell of her. She left today."

If anything, his mother sounded pleased at the blow she was dealing him.

"What do you mean, she left? Where is she? Where has she gone?"

"She expressed a desire to return to her family in England. It was a natural enough request to make. I saw no reason to refuse her."

No wonder his mother had forgiven him for capturing Louisa, now that she was gone beyond his reach. "You helped her to escape."

"Was this riad to be her home, or to be her prison?" The question cut him like a whip.

"You helped her."

"She was determined to go. I saw that she was protected on the way."

The news struck him with the force of a bullet between the eyes. She had gone. Louisa, his woman, his bride, had left him. She had chosen to spurn everything he offered her and run away like a thief in the night, as though he meant nothing to her—less than nothing. And his own mother had helped her on her way. "I will never forgive you for your betrayal."

"I have been a woman longer than I have been a mother," she replied staunchly, holding her ground against his fury. "I could not stand by and see her unhappy."

He put his head in his hands so his mother could not see the desolation in his face. "How could she be unhappy? She had everything that a woman could want. I gave her everything."

"Everything except her freedom." She laid a pitying hand on his head, as if he were ten years old again and was crying over a broken toy. "In the end, that was all that mattered to her."

Nine

Louisa sat upright on the straight-backed chair, her hands folded primly in her lap. Her high-necked gray gown was practically buttoned up to her chin, and her hair was dressed in a severe chignon. Her smile, as false as the string of pearls she wore around her neck, was wearing thin. Never, even as a hired nursemaid, had she felt so ill at ease in company before.

Caroline and Beatrice did their best, but her sisters could not always be by her side, and as soon as she was alone, the vultures descended once more.

The women were not so bad; though some of them looked askance at her and made audible comments about her loose morals, most of them were content to leave her in peace. It was the men who caused her the most grief.

Despite the deliberate plainness and severity of her dress, it seemed every disreputable man in the district had heard rumors of her time spent in the harem of a powerful bey in Morocco, and they were eager to try their own luck with her.

None of them offered to lead her out onto the dance floor— she was not the sort of respectable young woman with whom they could dance. Their offers were far more direct and made with little pretense of politeness. Mr. Anstruthers offered to show her around the conservatory that, he pronounced with a smarmy leer, was quite unlit at this time of the evening. Mr. Convers, who was married and had a brood of children, whispered in her ear an invitation to take her to a music hall that had not even been vaguely respectable for years. Mr. Fibberts, an acknowledged rake, offered her the post of governess in his household, though he had only one child, an infant of just a few weeks old.

Eventually she had endured enough of such unsubtle attempts to woo her. She had suffered through an evening in company—surely that would be enough to salve Caroline's conscience and silence those who might accuse her sisters of doing too little to integrate her back into society. No one could accuse her of trying to hide out in the country and avoid the local gentry. She had outfaced them all for several hours and she was weary of the effort.

Rising from her chair, she sidled out the closest door and onto the balcony, shutting the door behind her. What a relief it was to be away from the cloying atmosphere of the drawing room, even though the outside air was cold and damp and made her cough. The air in Morocco had been so much warmer and drier than it was here in England. The nighttime air there had not caught in her lungs as the air did here, even during the day. She had not felt perfectly well ever since she had gotten on board the leaky tub that had carried her away from the heat and color of Morocco and back to the cold, gray shores of England.

She took out her handkerchief to muffle the noise of her coughing. The last thing she wanted was to draw any unwelcome attention out here in the peaceful garden. She had suffered more than enough of that inside.

Late-blooming roses carried their faint scent through the still evening air. Leaning against the balcony, she inhaled deeply, trying not to cough again as the cold air penetrated her lungs. She'd always loved the smell of roses. They grew everywhere in Morocco, for distilling into rose water for use in their perfumes and in their delicious sweets. It had been one of the things she had loved best about living there. The glorious perfumes, the spices, the heat . . .

And Khair Bey, she reminded herself with a little shake. Khair Bey, who had manipulated her and lied to her in the worst possible way. Khair Bey, who had tricked her into thinking she was his slave, who had made her his mistress with no compunction and no remorse. Even if the rest of Morocco was peopled with angels, they could not make amends for his wickedness.

No, England was her home, not Morocco. She would have

to become accustomed to her own country once more, and stop this foolish longing for a place where she did not belong— where she would never belong.

The sound of quiet footsteps on the balcony was the only warning she got that she was no longer alone. Resolutely, she kept her back turned to the intruder, hoping he would get the message that she wanted to be left alone.

He didn't take the hint. Coming up closely behind her, he placed one arm on either side of her, pinning her to the balcony with the weight of his body. His breath, stinking of port wine and brandy, was hot on her neck. "Ah ha, so I have caught the elusive Miss Clemens at last," he said with a throaty chuckle. "I thought I would never get the chance to find you alone, and that some other man would beat me to the prize."

She twisted her head around to face her attacker. Ugh. It was Mr. Capill who had collared her, a middle-aged gentleman with a red face and a paunch. "Let me go," she said calmly, though she was feeling far from calm. His bulk intimidated her and crowded her, and she found it hard to breathe.

"There's no need to be so hoity-toity with me," he said, moving one of his hands to paw at her breasts. "Not when I know where you've been and what you've been doing while you were there."

"I have been a nursery maid in Italy," she said stoutly, pushing his hand away firmly. "It was a respectable position with a respectable family." Her stay in Khair Bey's casbah was nobody's business but her own, and all she wanted was to forget it as soon as she could. It certainly was none of Mr. Capill's business.

"That's not all you were doing, though, was it, dearie?" He bent his head and nuzzled fat, wet lips on her neck. "You were in a harem in Morocco, the plaything of a Moroccan prince, until he tired of you. Did you learn all the tricks of the harem women while you were there? What did they teach you? Did they give you some fancy new Eastern tricks to share? Did you learn how to make a man faint with pleasure in your arms?"

The time for politeness was passed. He would not leave her alone. Louisa drew back her elbow and jabbed it sharply into his gut as hard as she could. "That is no excuse for you to behave as if I were a loose woman. I am a respectable Englishwoman, and no man's toy. I was not his, and I am certainly not yours."

He gave a grunt of pain and stumbled to his knees. "You can try and put a brave face on it, but everyone knows you were nothing more than a willing slut for a dirty foreigner," he spat as he clambered to his feet again, winded by the blow. "You ought to be grateful that an Englishman is prepared to take you to his bed at all, after letting a foreigner meddle with you. Most people would be too finicky to take you on, even as a bought-and-paid-for mistress, but I've always had a taste for the exotic. I like to sample everything on offer, no matter where it's been before me."

His words cut into her like a knife. Was this what they thought of her, these English people who had come bearing false words of sympathy for her ordeal, meanwhile pumping her for every last detail of harem life? That she was irredeemably spoiled goods—easy pickings for any man prepared to overlook her dalliance with a foreigner?

With a look of pure disdain, she left him still breathing heavily with pain on the balcony and went back inside, her appetite for revelry completely gone. All she wanted to do was go home and lick her wounds in private. Morocco might not have been her home, but it seemed that England was even less so.

Beatrice clearly had been looking for her. She hurried over to Louisa's side as soon as she caught sight of her. "You are pale. Are you feeling well?"

"I am tired." Louisa explained her paleness with a convenient excuse. There was no point in letting Beatrice know just how badly Mr. Capill had made her feel. Though younger than her by more than a year, Beatrice had always been her fiercest protector and her champion.

Mr. Capill surely would not be the last to proposition her so openly. At least he had the courage, or the lack of tact, to put into words what everyone else in her acquaintance was surely thinking. They despised her for her amour with Khair Bey, when in truth, he was worth twenty of any of them. Though he had lied to her and betrayed her, he treated his own people with love and affection. He would never turn on any of his people with such viciousness, whatever they had done.

Beatrice pressed her hand warmly. "I, too, am tired of the company. I will find Caroline and her husband and ask them to bring the carriage around right away."

Louisa smiled gratefully at her sister. Beatrice had always cared for her, ever since she was tiny. Thankfully there were still a few people in England who loved her and wished her well.

Khair Bey stood on the ramparts of the wall surrounding his village and looked out toward the horizon—toward the coast, where his Louisa had set sail three weeks and five days ago. In his fervor he had pursued her that far, only to discover she had found passage on a boat to England that had departed only a few hours before. She had left him, betrayed him, and he was desolate without her. His meat had no flavor and no water could quench his thirst. Without Louisa beside him, the home of his childhood felt like the house of a stranger, and the land of his fathers appeared a barren, desolate desert.

He clenched his fists together so tightly that his nails dug into his palms. His craving for her was a weakness that he needed to expel. It clouded his wits and dulled his mind, made him heavy when he ought to be light, and poisoned him with despair.

It was nothing but callow foolishness to hanker after a woman who cared nothing for him, to waste his soul with regrets and blight his life with wanting. He had loved her, but she had run from him. He should expunge her from his life as ruthlessly as she had done with him. Only when he had utterly forgotten her—the sound of her voice, the feeling of her body against him, the light in her eyes, and the sparkle of her smile—would he be himself again.

But even though each memory of her tormented him beyond bearing, he could not forget.

His mother came up behind him, almost noiselessly on her slippered feet. "If you truly love her, you should go after her. It is not too late."

"Were it not for you, there would be no need," he reminded her cruelly. "You took her from me."

"Her unhappiness was not of my doing. Once she knew the truth of her capture, she did not want to stay."

Sometimes, on a clear day, he could almost see the blue of the ocean from here, and smell the salt on the air. "Then what is the point of following? So she can reject me again?" It hurt enough to be rejected once. If she were to turn her back on him a second time, he was not sure he could survive the blow. "A man has his pride."

His mother's sigh disappeared into the wind. "A man can have too much pride when it interferes with what he really wants. Put aside your pride for once, my son, or you will doom yourself to a life of regret."

The plains in front of him were well tended—the olive trees were laden with fruit and the wheat had grown high. The harvest would be good again this year, and he along with his entire village would prosper. But none of it meant anything to him anymore. What use was wealth if he had no one to spend it on?

He would give it all away if only Louisa would come back to him. "If she had wanted me, she would have stayed. Now that she is in England with her family, what hope do I have of bringing her back here? I can offer her nothing that she wants. There is nothing to tempt her back to me."

"You can offer her your love."

"To have her spit it back in my face? I do not think so."

Layla sat down by his side on a bench built into the ramparts and gazed down at the plains. The sun beat down on their backs and sent shimmers of hazy heat dancing over the fields of wheat. "She is in love with you, you know," she said softly. "I suspect she is missing you quite as badly as you are missing her."

"Her actions would suggest otherwise," he said acerbically. Women, even his mother, could be such fools, believing what they wanted to believe rather than the truth that was staring them in the face. If Louisa had felt anything at all for him, she would not have left.

"She told me so," his mother's voice was imbued with sadness, "the night before she left."

It hurt him too much to hear it, to think that she could love him and yet leave him anyway. If she had loved him enough, she would have stayed. "She was lying."

"I do not think so. She loves you, but she hated herself for loving you. Being your mistress—and not your wife—cheapened her in her own eyes. Even as she took great pleasure in lying with you, she hated herself for her enjoyment."

"I would have married her if she had stayed. From the beginning I meant to have her as my wife. I never would have brought her here otherwise."

His mother sighed deeply. "You should have married her in Italy. That would have been easier on both of you."

He shook his head in silence. Louisa would never have wed him then, even if he had pushed the matter. Morocco had been a mystery to her then, and she had known nothing of the life she would lead as his wife. It would have been asking too much of her to leap into the unknown with a man she barely knew.

"She wants to love you, but in a way that will allow her to love herself, too." She stood up and put her arm around his shoulders. "That is all she needs. You can give her that, if you choose to."

His mother's embrace removed some of the sadness from his soul. Maybe she knew Louisa better than he did. Maybe there was still hope—a way to make things right.

"There is always hope." She spoke as if she had read the doubts plaguing his mind. "Go after her, son. Tell her that you are miserable without her, that the sun does not shine on you when she is gone. Let her know that you were wrong to take away her freedom, and that you will never do so again. Then she will come to you, willingly, and she will truly be your woman."

Louisa sat in the parlor staring silently out at the weather. Beatrice had been obliged to return to London where she was training to become a nurse at St. Thomas's Hospital, and her departure had left Louisa dull and depressed. She missed her younger sister so much that she would almost be tempted to join her in her training, but the mere thought of having to mop up blood and empty bedpans made her ill.

It was raining again, and the sky was a deep, sullen gray. Though it was barely four in the afternoon, Caroline had already lit the gas lamps to give them enough light to see by.

The trees along the avenue were bowed down from the rain, their leaves and branches drooping, and water dripping off them as if they were weeping. The front lawn where the children played had all but disappeared into a morass of mud, and the wooden garden benches were so waterlogged that a fragile layer of green moss had started to creep over every surface.

She coughed in a desultory fashion, barely having the energy needed to clear the damp from her lungs. It was at times like this that she missed Morocco most: the heat and the dust that seemed to get everywhere, into every crevice and cranny, no matter how you wrapped yourself up against it; the bright sunshine over the olive groves; and the cool water of the river at the bottom of the valley.

A gardener squelched past the window in a pair of sturdy boots, his footsteps leaving great sinkholes in the mud. A great sigh escaped her at the sight. She did not know how Caroline managed to keep her good health, or her spirits, in such an evil climate as England possessed.

Caroline laid down her pen and pushed her account books aside. "You are not happy back in England."

Louisa shook her head, but not with any great enthusiasm. The patter of the rain on the roof beat out an insistent rhythm that seemed as though it would never leave her in peace again. "I am very glad to see all my family again. I missed you all."

"But you do not like England, nonetheless."

"The sky is so gray," she admitted. "It is always cloudy and it rains so often." She shuddered and drew her shawl even more tightly around her shoulders. Though a fire burned brightly in the fireplace, sparking and hissing away, the slabs of pine piled in the grate provided little warmth. She had not been warm for a moment since she had set foot on the shore. "I had forgotten how cold it can be here in late autumn."

"You are spoiled from your time in Italy. The weather so far has been unseasonably mild."

"Maybe I have been." She sighed. It was not Italy she was pining for, but the blue skies and warm sun of Morocco. Even as a captive in Morocco, she had known more happiness than as a free woman in England.

Khair Bey had been fond of her and had looked after her well. Why hadn't that been enough for her? Why had she resolved to throw all she had away because she did not have everything she wanted?

Was her freedom worth that much to her? Or was her love worth more?

At the first sting of betrayal, she had left him with no thought of ever returning. But now she missed his presence by her side, she missed the warmth of his laughter, the kindness of his touch. She missed lying beside him at night, a thin silk coverlet all that was needed to keep off the cool night air. Worst of all, she missed his kisses, the touch of his hands on her body, and the thickness of him as he pressed inside her. It was shameless of her, she knew, but she missed her lover.

Caroline took her by the hand. "If you miss him that much, Louisa," she said firmly, "you should go back to him. Life is not worth living without the man you love by your side. I almost lost Dominic before I realized that truth."

"He bought and sold me as if I were nothing, as if I did not have a soul. How can I forgive him for that?"

"Didn't Dominic do the same with me?" Caroline smiled in remembrance. "I gave myself to him for the price of being rescued from the workhouse. It did not stop me from falling in love with him—or him with me. And now I am a respectable married woman with a house in the country, as if I had never been Dominic's mistress before I became his wife."

"Dominic is in love with you." Even after so many years together, it was plain that he still doted on his wife, and she on him. She envied the happiness they had found together. "He won you, even though all seemed lost."

"You ran away from Ithry Khair to regain your freedom," her sister reminded her. "Isn't it possible that he, too, is feeling hurt and betrayed?"

"You are on his side. You think I should forgive him for what he did to me?" She pulled away from her sister and strode over to the window. It was raining again, as it always was in England. Oh, how she longed to feel the sun on her face once more. She hated this country with a passion. "It was unforgivable. Even if he were to crawl to me on his hands and knees begging for forgiveness, I could not grant it to him."

"Do not twist my words. I know he is unworthy of you and I am on no one's side but the side of happiness. I see you pining away, hardly eating, walking around with a face as long as one of my basset hounds. I would welcome the devil himself if he would make you smile again."

Louisa stared out of the window, watching a drop of rain as it shimmered down a branch and then fell with a plop onto a puddle of water on the graveled driveway. "I left him without a word, without even a note to tell him where I had gone, or why. It was wrong of me." The wind whistled hollowly around the edge of the house, echoing the desolation of her thoughts.

"If I could go back to him not as a slave but as a free woman, I would return to him in a heartbeat." Her voice faded into a tiny murmur. "I would return even as his captive, if he would have me no other way." There, she had confessed the deepest shame in her soul. She would rather be Ithry Khair's captive than the wife of any other man in Christendom—or out of it.

"Go to him then," Caroline counseled her, coming up behind Louisa and putting an arm around her shoulder. "Tell him so. If he loves you in return, he will welcome you back with open arms."

"And if he does not want me?" She could not speak above a whisper. It was her most secret fear that in her absence he had found another woman to take to his bed, another woman to love. She would rather die at once than be faced with his infidelity. "What if he has found another woman? One who will not demand more of him than he is willing to give? One who will forgive him when he wrongs her?"

"Are you willing to take that chance? Or would you rather live with your regrets for the rest of your life?"

"But what if I am too late?" she wailed. "What shall I do then?"

Caroline grimaced at the thought. "If your Moroccan prince has found another woman, then, somehow or other, you will have to make your peace with England."

Louisa watched another drop of rain run down the windowpane. There really was no choice to be made. She could return to Morocco and take a chance on life, or stay in England and die.

Just a few days later, Louisa sat on the train to Bristol, a small portmanteau at her feet and the weight of England off her shoulders. In the morning, at Avonmouth Docks in the Port of Bristol, a steamship that plied the route between there and Morocco was due to arrive. As soon as she got to Bristol, she would purchase herself a ticket. When the steamship left England, she would be on board.

Even the thought of the impending sea voyage could not dim her excitement. She was going home.

By the time the train pulled into the station at Bristol, it was too late to do anything but hail a cab to take her to a quiet hotel.

Early the next morning, she made her way to the docks, even though the steamer was not expected until midday. Although a young clerk at the steamship company had booked her a passage, she would not risk having her journey to Morocco delayed by relying solely on his word that there would be a cabin free for her. Steamers to Morocco were infrequent enough that she did not want to miss the sailing.

With his spotty face and trousers that did not quite reach his ankles, the clerk did not look above sixteen years of age. She had even hesitated to entrust him with her money. It was imperative that she speak with the captain as soon as he arrived in order to confirm her passage.

Right at midday, the steamship arrived as scheduled. She had to marvel at the precision of the engineering that removed the vagaries of weather from their schedule—vagaries often suffered by sailing ships.

Standing on the dock, she joined the bustling crowd that had gathered to watch the newfangled steamer come into port. Around her, fellow travelers and well-wishers mingled with traders, gawkers, and locals touting accommodation, food, and other services that sailors and visitors seek while in port.

There was a sense of excitement as the ship came alongside, with burly wharfies handling the heavy ropes, tying the vessel to the large yellow bollards that lined the edge of the dock. Finally, the gangway was lowered from the ship, and the many travelers jostled their way down the steep stairway, eager to be off the ship after the days at sea. Some faces were still tinged with green. Louisa watched them disembark with empathy; she liked the sea no more than they.

Mostly men, they wore hats that were a symbol of their class. Poorer men wore flat caps and sailors wore woolen caps, while the more well-to-do gentlemen wore top hats—all were the same dreary black or dark gray. No color at all, nothing to stand out in this dull, dreary country.

Then at the top of the gangway appeared a splash of color, the brightness of a red fez worn by a Moroccan man. She couldn't help but smile at the memory. How she loved the warmth and color, the life of her adopted country.

The man in the red fez turned toward her as he strode onto the gangway. Her heart seemed to stop in her chest, her breath caught in her throat, and for a moment she thought she would faint. As the wearer of the fez strode down the gangway and out of the shadows, the unmistakable face of Ithry Khair was revealed in the noon light.

On its own volition, her body started moving toward the bottom of the gangway, and she elbowed her way relentlessly through the crowds. Seeing his face had brought back so many happy memories: warm sunshine and spicy food, intelligent conversation, and his strong hands caressing her body. Her heart was racing with the thought of being in his arms again.

Eventually, her progress was blocked by the throngs at the bottom of the gangway, as the weary travelers clashed head-on with their welcoming parties. She could get no closer to him until he came to her.

She paused in the middle of the crowd, suddenly assailed by a fearful doubt. What was she thinking? What if he was here for business, and had not come for her? What would she say? Should she hide in the anonymity of the crowds?

No, her heart would not allow her to retreat. She would be brave and fight for what she wanted. And what she wanted most of all was him.

With renewed strength she continued on, forcing her way the last short distance to the gangway, terrified now that she would miss him in the milling crowd. If she were to lose him in this melee, she would never find him again.

Bursting out from between two large portly men, she reached the bottom of the gangway just as Ithry stepped off. The surging crowds pushed them together, as if willing them with a mass consciousness to find each other once more.

The two of them stood there among the sea of moving people. She could not speak, and even if she could have forced words over the lump in her throat, she had no words to say. She gazed mutely into his face, registering his surprise, his astonishment, and then the growing delight in his eyes.

With the crowd still swirling around them, he put out one hand and touched her on the cheek, as if he could hardly trust the evidence of his senses—as though he did not believe she was really standing there in front of him.

He smiled at her then, a smile that came from his soul. "Such beauty have I rarely seen in thousands of miles of travel across oceans and distant lands," he whispered. "I am captive in your presence." Then he dropped his bags and took her in his arms, oblivious to the curses of those around him.

Louisa nestled in his arms, her heart singing with joy. Finally, she was where she belonged. "And I am captive in yours."

Arm in arm, they walked away from the docks, moving westward toward the hills of Clifton that beckoned them with the promise of green.

He held her tightly, as if he feared to let her go. "How could you know to find me here? My mother was the only one who knew I was coming to England. I told no one else, for fear that I would fail in my mission and return home empty-handed."

She was still giddy with the shock of seeing him again, of having her arm tucked into his, of walking by his side. "I did not know you were on the boat. I had booked a passage on it for myself."

He stopped for a moment and looked into her eyes, fearing to believe her, searching her face for the truth. "You were coming back to Morocco? Back to me?"

"I missed you," she said simply.

"It is more than I deserve." By now they had reached a park, a small oasis of green in the middle of the bustling port city. He led her to a park bench, where they sat together, side by side, his arm around her shoulders. Louisa nestled into his side. He had brought the warmth of Morocco to England with him, making even foggy Bristol come alive with sunshine.

His voice was low with shame when he spoke again. "I have wronged you, Louisa. And I have come to confess to my failings and to beg your forgiveness."

He was a proud man, and she knew the effort it must have cost him to ask her pardon. She reached out and stroked his cheek with the back of her hand. "You do not need to."

"I wronged you far more than I wanted to admit to myself. You were happy in Italy, and I pursued you relentlessly. My only excuse, and a feeble excuse it was, was that I wanted you too much to leave you be. I made your position there so uncomfortable that you had to leave."

"I would have had to leave soon anyway," Louisa reminded him gently. "The girls no longer needed a nursemaid."

He shook his head at her attempt to reassure him. "You are kinder to me than I deserve. You have always been kinder to me than I deserve. Even when you made your wishes clear by running away from me, I had my men pursue your ship and take you captive. I led you to believe that you were a slave, and that you belonged to me. I took away your freedom, you ability to determine your own fate."

How could she have thought to live without him? "My fate was determined when I first met you." She could not be happy without this strong, proud man beside her.

"I know that you value your freedom, Louisa, and you have my word that I will never take it from you. But I have to know the truth—can there be any place for me in your life?" He stopped short and swallowed, before visibly steeling himself to continue. "If you say no, I will respect your decision. Even I can learn from my mistakes. I will not force you into something you do not want."

"There will always be a place for you in my life." She laid a hand on his chest to feel his heart beat, knowing that it beat for her. "I love you, Ithry."

His heart jumped under her hand. "You really love me? You do not hold my foolishness against me?"

"I have always loved you. And I have long forgiven any hurt you did to me."

He captured her glance with his, and truth sparkled bright in his dark eyes. "You will not regret your decision, I promise you. I will make my home in England, if that is what you desire. Anywhere, as long as we can be together."

She shuddered at the thought of having to stay in England, where it was so damp and cold, and she felt so out of place and lonely. "Not England. Anywhere but England. I have missed Morocco so much. I would like to go back there with you."

"You will come back with me to my homeland?"

She slipped her hand into his. "I thought you would never ask."

With one fluid movement, he sank to one knee in front of her, ignoring the whistle of amusement he received from a passing street urchin. "There is only one more thing I need to make my happiness complete. Louisa, will you do me the honor of becoming my wife?"

Before she could answer, he drew a small box from his pocket and flipped it open to reveal a huge diamond solitaire. "I wanted to marry you back in Italy, but I did not dare to ask as I feared you would refuse me. I wanted to bind you to me forever, to possess you without any risk to my pride. It was arrogant and foolish of me. But now I ask you, with nothing but my love to recommend me, to marry me."

Her fingers shaking, Louisa accepted the ring and allowed him to place it on her finger. "I have always loved you, and I always will. You have given me the gift of choice, and with it, I choose you."

A few days later, after a smooth sea voyage and bumpy ride on the back of a donkey across the hills of the Rif, they arrived back at the Khair Bey's casbah. Louisa rode into the gates at his side, feeling as if she had finally come home.

The women of the household were all waiting for them in the courtyard, smiles stretching from ear to ear. At their entrance, the women all broke into happy twittering and Layla clasped Louisa in her arms with a joyous laugh. "You came back with

Ithry. I am so glad for both of you. I so hoped you would come back."

"How could I do otherwise?" Louisa spread her hand out to display the thin gold band she wore on her finger. "A newly married bride cannot forsake her husband."

"We did not want to linger in England, and I could not wait to wed her until we returned home," Khair Bey explained. "I had the ship's captain marry us."

"Then you are back to stay? Of your own free will."

Louisa gave a smile that radiated all the joy she felt in her heart. "Of my own free will I am back to stay. Forever."

LEDA SWANN is the writing duet of Cathy and Brent. They write out of their home overlooking the sea in peaceful New Zealand. When not writing they have busy lives working in the technology industry, bringing up four children, and enjoying an adventurous outdoor life that ranges from the mountains to the sea.

Leda Swann